MARR

C000218256

She was twenty-five, qualified in medicine and surgery and afraid of no man. So why did Gabrielle let her boss, the well-known woman-hater Dr Robert Scorer, shatter her calm and throw her love life into a hopeless tangle?

MARRYING A DOCTOR

BY
ELIZABETH HARRISON

MILLS & BOON LIMITED
15–16 BROOK'S MEWS
LONDON W1A 1DR

First published in Great Britain 1984
by Robert Hale Limited
This edition published 1985
by Mills & Boon Limited

© Elizabeth Harrison 1984

Australian copyright 1985
Philippine copyright 1985

ISBN 0 263 75022 1

Set in 11 on 12½ pt Linotron Times
03–0485–40,332

Photoset by Rowland Phototypesetting Ltd
Bury St Edmunds, Suffolk
Made and printed in Great Britain by
Richard Clay (The Chaucer Press) Ltd
Bungay, Suffolk

CHAPTER ONE

A SLIGHT figure in her working outfit of denim skirt and waistcoat over a plain cream blouse, her white coat left behind in Outpatients, Gabrielle Vereker walked purposefully along the corridor towards the director's office.

To feel panicky was absurd. All she was going to do was to issue an informal invitation to a party that evening. If he didn't choose to accept it, no one could care less. So why was she in this state of jitters? Perhaps she should give up the idea of inviting him, especially as everyone obviously considered her crazy even to contemplate it. But she couldn't forget that when dear old Uncle Fred had been director he'd always been the first to be invited to any celebration. Now Uncle Fred had gone, his place taken by this quelling stranger with a bleak eye and a voice to match.

Perhaps the others were right. Robert Scorer, if he condescended to show up at all, would only cast a total frost over the evening.

Hell, no. The director had always been invited to unit parties, and he wasn't going to be left out now, whatever anyone said. This could be a test case. If he turned this invitation of hers down, no one need invite him to anything ever again.

Her eyes sparking, she braced slim shoulders,

set a mouth more often softness itself. She was twenty-five, qualified in medicine and surgery, afraid of no man. She knocked smartly on the door, opened it immediately and sailed in, dark head high.

Robert Scorer had his back to her. A fine beginning. He didn't bother to turn round, either, merely grunted enquiringly.

'Nothing urgent or important.' Gabrielle was infuriated to find herself uttering this hesitant phrase. 'I just wanted to let you know we're having a party this evening.'

Presumably having at last completed whatever it was he'd been so engrossed in, he turned round from the side table scattered with books and journals and crossed to his desk. Tall and angular, dark-haired, with smouldering brown eyes instead of Uncle Fred's blue twinkle, he had a long overbearing nose for looking down and a narrow mouth only too often, they had discovered, compressed with rage. Gabrielle was certainly not alone in fearing him. Accustomed to genial Uncle Fred, the unit frequently found their new director alarming.

He sat down at his desk, pulled his note pad towards him. Blasted parties. Unfortunately, he reminded himself, as the director he probably ought to put in an appearance. 'What time?' he snapped.

'A—about seven-thirty.'

'Where?'

'In my flat.' She told him the address, and explained how to get there.

He grunted. 'What's it in aid of?'

'Well, actually it's a sort of engagement party.' To her increasing fury, she could hear a note of apology in her voice.

'An engagement party?' Hell, he'd have to show up. So who, among this new staff of his, was getting engaged? 'Whose?'

'Well, mine, in fact.'

'Oh. Er—congratulations. Who'—the cliché came grinding out as if it repelled him, as indeed it did—'who's the lucky man?'

'Dr Singh, actually.'

'But he can't be.' Paul Singh was Robert Scorer's registrar, and he was well enough acquainted with him to know that he had no right to be getting engaged to anyone in the hospital. 'He's got a fiancée in India,' he said baldly. 'Told me so himself. Arranged marriage—family affair.'

Now what had she got into? Who'd have guessed that the remote, unapproachable Robert Scorer, of all people, would have at his fingertips the details of Paul's marriage plans? And why, if he already knew about the arranged marriage, hadn't Paul brought him up to date? 'He's written breaking it off,' she explained unwillingly. 'And I did say it's only a sort of engagement party. Not an official one. Nor an official engagement at all. We just thought we'd like to drink to our future together, with'—she swallowed—'with our friends.'

'Up to you.' He was dismissive. 'Ask me, you're jumping the gun a bit. What's more, you ought to be concentrating on your work for the Membership, not throwing parties.'

'If that's how you feel, please don't dream of coming,' Gabrielle retorted. 'Sorry I bothered you.' She stepped back through the door, closed it with extreme care so that there was no chance whatever of its banging, and walked away along the corridor. Thank you for nothing, Dr Robert Scorer. As far as I'm concerned, you can get lost for ever. A pity she'd made the effort to ask him. Better if she'd left it alone. The others had been right.

Luckily he didn't matter that to her. She flicked her fingers in mid-air, considerably astonishing two staff nurses who came hurtling round the corner as she did it.

In his office, Robert Scorer was frowning, annoyed with himself. He'd handled that about as badly as he could have done. He sighed wearily. Now he was director of the unit, he had to pull himself together, make a real attempt to refrain from blurting out whatever came into his head. What a hopeless waste, though. Dr Vereker—Gabrielle, he remembered, that was her name—Dr Gabrielle Vereker was a lovely and brilliant girl, poised, he would have assumed (had he bothered to think about it, which normally he wouldn't have done) for an outstanding career and, one day, marriage to another top consultant. Instead, here she was, ready to throw herself away on Paul Singh. A nice enough lad—an exceptionally nice lad, in fact—but dull as last week's papers. A good, competent registrar, trustworthy and hardworking, who would mature into an equally good general practitioner. He'd never make any hideous errors, since, cautious as well as kind, he could recognise his own limitations, and knew when to seek advice. A thoroughly worthy young man, no one would deny it, but Gabrielle Vereker would be wasting her potential if she went into general practice with him.

And then there was this additional complication of the arranged marriage in India.

Robert Scorer swore.

There was nothing he could do about any of it, though. So he might as well forget it. It was nothing to do with him. He was the director of the unit, not a marriage broker.

The thought brought him up suddenly against a memory, and for the first time he understood his own chief's reactions when, nearly ten years ago, he had announced his impending marriage to Lucilla. He remembered how the old man's face had changed when he heard the news, and how at intervals he'd ventured cagey little warning phrases, about young doctors not rushing into early marriages. The long absences from home, unpredictable, destructive, could place great strains on a marriage, he'd pointed out more than once. Early marriages were a mistake.

He could say that again, Robert thought caustically, staring unseeingly at the opposite wall. His own had been the height of idiocy. He'd been infatuated, that was all, had fallen like a goon for a pretty face and a sexy body, and failed to spot the empty mind. And exactly as they had tried to warn him, his marriage and his career had crashed in headlong collision. It had been the marriage that had ended.

Looking back now, he could understand that the disaster had been his fault quite as much as Lucilla's. At the time, though, he had not seen it like that. He'd blamed Lucilla for everything. Spoilt, inconsiderate, childish, she'd made no attempt to adjust. It had been his life he'd expected her to adapt to, of course. The demands of the hospital. Long hours, unforeseen absences, meals she had to put back, meals he'd never eaten, and —worst of all—the fact that he consistently failed, ever, to put her first.

He drummed irritated fingers on the desk. No use brooding over past anguish. None of this had anything to do with Gabrielle Vereker. He might not himself approve of her marriage to Paul Singh, but however it turned out it would be nothing like his own to Lucilla.

Banging drawers savagely, he cleared his desk and went off to Outpatients, where Paul Singh awaited him. His scowling chief gave him a rough ride all afternoon.

Gabrielle went through her own afternoon's work in the ward with verve and efficiency, though she was perhaps unusually brisk.

The staff, however, smiled, and caught one another's eye tolerantly. She had her party that evening, after all. Her *engagement* party. The entire Child Health Research Unit—apart, that is, from its director—had been watching and waiting, tenderly and hopefully, for months while Gabrielle Vereker and Paul Singh fell steadily and helplessly in love. Now, at last, they'd made it. The unit was delighted.

Gabrielle left punctually to reach the baker before he closed. She collected her order of fresh bread and new rolls, rushed on round the corner to her basement flat, and clambered carefully down the area steps clutching her paper bags, unlocked her own front door and went in.

  She cherished her flat. She had taken it over just as the previous owner had completed a face lift— the conversion of the narrow cupboard kitchen into an effective open-plan galley off the sitting room, and the ripping out of the basement stairs for a spacious hallway. At this point, she had explained sadly to Gabrielle, both money and time had run out, and she was off to a hospital post in Exeter. Given this head start, though, Gabrielle had paved what had until then been no more than a derelict yard shaded by an old London plane tree, whitewashed the surrounding walls, put up trellis and planted variegated ivy, which flourished and spread indomitably. She bought tubs for the new patio, planted them with trailing pink geraniums and fuchsia, and finally, this summer, she'd acquired garden chairs and a wrought-iron table. Here in the heart of the city she had an extra outdoor room open to the sky above and the song of the birds living in the great old London plane.

This evening the heat of the day was already lifting, a soft breeze rustled in the ivy and played with the fuchsia bells.

What she had to do, though, was to get cracking. She went into her shining kitchen, piled the still-warm rolls on to their wicker baskets, cut the crusty bread into thick slices, divided the savoury quiches she'd made last night—cheese and onion, asparagus, bacon and tomato—and piled the squares on to plates, put out her bowls of dip, the butter, the cheese boards, celery in the cut-glass tumblers that had been her grandmother's pride. She looked round, checking, and nodded to herself. It would do. The room was welcoming and filled with bowls of summer flowers—Canterbury bells, scabious, marguerites, larkspur. Party spirit filled her with anticipation, and she was only mildly put out when Paul telephoned to say he'd be late.

'One of the family doctors has just rung in to say he has a child—a kid from the asthma research project—with a severe attack. He wants her admitted, so I'll have to wait here until he arrives with her.'

'Never mind,' Gabrielle said easily. 'Come as soon as you can.' All in the day's work, she thought, as she put the telephone down. And it didn't really matter. She and her flat were ready and in party mood.

She'd be sad to leave here. The idea upset her, but she pushed it hastily away. In future, life was going to be unimaginably better. Their plans, hers and Paul's, involved giving up this flat, but so what? She was going to marry Paul and move to Ledford, a town in the midlands, where she would take a registrar's post, they had agreed, in the local hospital for two years, and then join him in practice with his uncle and aunt in the town until they started their family. An end to loneliness.

Ever since her grandmother had died she'd been searingly lonely. She'd battled on, qualified and done well, but there'd been no Gran to enjoy her triumph, and there never would be again. Gran had gone for ever. Soon, though, she'd belong again. Not only to Paul, so gentle, kindly and sheltering, but also to his family. She'd have a true home again.

A sense of adventure spurred her on, too. Paul's Indian family would open wider horizons. She'd move into a different world. With him, she would be making a new sort of marriage.

Against all this, the passing sadness of leaving this flat of hers had to be pushed on one side. It was, after all, only bricks and mortar—even if the bricks did date back, astonishingly, to 1720. She cast a final glance round the room, and went through to her minute bathroom to shower. Tepid water ran refreshingly down over her hot stickiness, and she revelled in it, turning her face up, letting liquid delight almost hypnotize her. The water ran along her arms, her legs, over her breasts, against her closed lids. She took in deep restoring breaths, and all at once longed for Paul.

Her eyes flew open, and she saw her pale slimness in the mirror. She ached for Paul to see her like this, naked and—surely?—beautiful, inviting. Surely he'd love her and want her if he saw her like this?

Paul was positively Edwardian.

He respected, he said, his affianced bride, exactly as he would have respected Anik. Anik was the girl in India to whom his family had engaged him, long years back. 'To me, you are in same position,' he told her seriously. 'I am not seeking cheap affair.'

So no sex before marriage. Paul had been hurt at the suggestion he might have had anything of the sort in mind. More than hurt, he'd been angry. He was usually so gentle, but he'd been angry with her.

She supposed she should have been flattered. Instead she, in her turn, was angry.

'My body is my own,' she'd told him hotly. 'Mine to do as I please. It's not some property that you'll have a right to after marriage. I give it to you whenever you wish, because I love you. It's part of me, and I choose to share it with you.'

He'd shaken his head, and said 'But I shan't allow you to. So that is that. It is wonderful, Gaby, that you wish this, and I love you for it. Even more. But I have to be strong for both of us'—'as a man should', luckily for him, remained unsaid—'and tell you that I have no intention of touching you until we are truly married.'

That appeared to be that.

Gabrielle drenched herself in the toilet water a grateful patient had given her, and scowled at her reflection.

Unwanted. Her body failed to turn him on.

Nonsense. She was being silly. After all, Gran would thoroughly have approved of his attitude. She had not been any sort of a prude, but she always asserted that relationships should be given a chance to develop before a couple fell into bed together. 'Nothing worthwhile was ever lost by waiting,' she used to say.

In any case, Gabrielle had to admit, if she was strictly honest, that she had mixed feelings on the subject. There were occasions, like this evening, when she wanted Paul to make love to her. She wanted them to know one another totally. Body and soul. She wanted to feel his hands on her own flesh, she wanted them to forget the world and the hospital in one another. She yearned for the union of their bodies, to add to the comfort of the emotional security they'd found together.

But there were other days when she actually treasured the barriers they'd established, when she was thankful to be able to call her body her own, invaded by no one, at the call of no man. She treasured, too, the quiet and gentle closeness she and Paul had so steadily built up. A spiritual affinity, not at the mercy of sexual demands, a warm and loving friendship, knowing nothing of the heights and depths of passionate intensity. This was what she needed.

Abruptly, staring at her own graceful nakedness, she frowned. Was this going to be enough?

It wouldn't have to be enough. Not once they were married. All they were doing, she and Paul, was to take life at what was the right pace for them. Building for a lifetime, slowly and surely.

In her bedroom her dress lay spread out on the bed. Beige silk, with that season's ruffles round the wide collar and on the narrow wrists. It had cost far too much, but—so Paul had assured her —it did amazing things for her, underlining, he'd said, her supple grace, exaggerating her slenderness. When she wore it, he told her, her breasts were more perfect than ever, and her lips far too alluring for comfort.

It had been delightful to listen to, even if he had still held to his unwelcome control. The memory, though, of his encouraging remarks gave her confidence, and she smiled at last, twitching a humorous eyebrow at the previously morose image in her dressing-table mirror. The image, of course, cheered up and grinned back, and she began to make up her face. She'd wear her hair loose this evening, she decided. Since she'd been qualified, she'd taken to wearing it in a knot at the nape of her neck. It made her look serious and older. More responsible. During her first days as a house physician she had more than once been taken for the ward clerk or the consultant's secretary rather than as a qualified doctor. For at twenty-five, Gabrielle, with her slight frame, her charmingly vulnerable features, her fast changing and easily read expressions, could be taken for a teenager— even so, as Paul would have pointed out, what a teenager. Quiet and understated, grey-eyed and dark-haired, she possessed in spite of everything an extraordinary capacity to make all those around her look undistinguished the moment she appeared. But of this she naturally had no suspicion herself, and this evening, as she brushed out her dark hair round beige silk shoulders, she shrugged, resigned, and told her reflection 'That's it. You'll have to do.'

She glanced at her watch. Ten minutes in hand. She wandered through the living room and out into the patio. All in order, ready and waiting.

She went in again, and poured the first glasses of wine. The bell rang.

On the doorstep Nicola, large, blonde and pregnant in a pretty flowery smock. 'I'm early, I know. But I thought I'd come straight in, in case you needed a hand. Andrew's parking the car.'

'Everything's ready, believe it or not. Come in, and have a drink.'

'Thanks. Bitter lemon for me, I'm afraid. I have to remember junior.'

'Sorry, I forgot.'

'Something I can never do.' She giggled cheerfully, and followed Gabrielle into the living room. 'It looks super, Gaby. Really super. I always loved this room, but it truly looks better than ever.'

'I was just thinking I shall be sorry to leave it,' Gabrielle admitted.

'Oh, must you? I suppose so, if you're going to Ledford. It does seem a shame.'

When they were both students, Nicola had shared the flat with Gabrielle, leaving it only on her marriage, by which stage Gabrielle, qualified and earning what seemed after all the penurious years a princely salary, had decided she could at last afford to run it on her own.

She and Nicola had been friends since the first days of their training, and it had been Nicola who had stoutly supported Gabrielle throughout the long years of her grandmother's increasing illness. Nicola had often put off dates—a luscious blonde, she could have gone out every night of the week with a different partner—to travel out to Stanmore on the underground and stay the night. She'd not only helped to cook, shop and sit with the invalid, who had grown very fond of her, but she regularly brought her notebooks with her, and took Gabrielle meticulously through the details of lectures and ward rounds she had been forced, during the last months of her grandmother's illness, to miss. Nicola, occupying a mixed flat in a tall house filled with students and young doctors, had been chased by hordes of eager young surgeons and doctors as well as her fellow students. Gabrielle, though, returning daily to Stanmore, had missed out on the casual dates and the budding romances, the excitement and the promise. She had lived only at second-hand, through Nicola. In return, she had seen Nicola through the ups and downs of her hectic love life, had finally encouraged her to marry Andrew. She'd been a bridesmaid at their wedding, had shopped with Nicola for carpets and curtains for their new home. Soon she would be godmother to their first child.

Bitter lemon in hand, Nicola wandered out to

the patio. 'I love your dress,' she told Gabrielle. 'Terrific. Must have cost a bomb—has expense written all over it.'

'You're right. It was a fearful price. I'd never have dreamt of buying it if Paul hadn't been urging me on. You really think—?' She looked enquiringly at Nicola. 'Worth it?'

'Every penny. Cross my heart. Where is Paul, anyway?'

'Oh, wouldn't you know? A problem in the ward. He'll be late.'

Nicola shrugged. 'Oh well, I suppose you should be thankful nothing cropped up to stop *you* getting away.' She sighed, and leant back luxuriantly. 'It's delicious out here, so cool, and this heavenly breeze. I think I shall stay out here all evening, trade on my condition and let everyone wait on me.' She extended a pair of legs once famous throughout the hospital, clad now in gossamer-thin pale pink tights and sandals, and sighed again. 'Perfect.'

The bell rang.

'Probably Andrew, if he's managed to park,' she said. 'Can I go on lolling here while you let him in?'

'Of course.'

It was Andrew, but hard on his heels down the area steps came half the unit, cheerful and exclaiming, and greeting Andrew and Nicola like friends lost for years, though in fact Andrew had taken up his senior registrar's post in a Hampshire hospital only eight months earlier.

The party was in full swing. Food and drink and

hospital gossip circulated, the door bell rang again and again. Gabrielle's engagement party was a success.

It lacked only her fiancé.

The late summer dusk had fallen before he came. Gabrielle had lighted candles in both the living room and the darkening garden. In the open, the flames burned steadily inside great globes of heavy Dartington glass, a recent birthday present from Andrew and Nicola.

'Gorgeous, aren't they?' Gabrielle gestured towards the flames. 'The finishing touch. Just as I imagined it could look out here.' She sat down at the table with the two of them. 'Thank you again.'

'It all looks great,' Nicola agreed. 'Tubs of flowers, garden furniture, and candlelight. All you need is a gaudy umbrella for the table. Your next birthday present, I promise.'

Gabrielle shook her head. 'Not a hope I'll still be here next summer.' She was curt.

Nicola and Andrew swivelled their heads in unison, and regarded her. Their eyes met.

Nicola spoke. 'Gaby, you are absolutely sure you—' She broke off, her eyes this time on the French windows. 'My God, who in the world is that? What a gorgeous hunk of man. Who is it? Since my time—I could never have overlooked him.'

Gabrielle stared reluctantly. Of all people, Robert Scorer was coming out into the patio, with Paul at his heels. 'Our new director.' She was short.

The two of them reached the table, and Paul began to apologize for being so late. Incredulously, Gabrielle heard her chief add his own apologies. 'Shocking to have kept Paul from his engagement party like this. You must have thought we were never going to show up, but we had quite a problem in the ward—still have, for that matter. I only looked in for a few minutes, I'm afraid.'

'I'll get you a drink,' Gabrielle said hastily.

When she returned, with drinks and a stand-by quiche she'd been hiding in the kitchen—the flat looked as though locusts had been through it—the four at the table were lost in discussion about the newly-admitted child. Robert Scorer took his glass from her absent-mindedly. 'Yes,' he was saying, 'Interesting in many ways. But damned dangerous. A good thing the family doctor had the sense to bring her straight in—she needs our facilities. Full laboratory back-up, radiography, piped oxygen. A ventilator at the ready in case we have to take over her breathing. I hope we shan't need to, but I'm bound to say I don't care for the look of her.'

'I'm surprised you felt able to come over here at all,' Gabrielle told him tartly.

'Oh, that was easy. We've left Chris sitting there, pushing in continuous adrenaline very slowly. He's got your number, anyway.'

'Just filling in time. I see.' Gabrielle nodded.

Robert Scorer nodded back at her, his confidence clearly unimpaired. 'Giving Chris a chance to get on with the job. No need to breathe down his neck. Counter-productive.' At this point he appeared to pick up Gabrielle's irritation. He read the cause for it unerringly. 'And it gives me an opportunity to wish you well,' he added smoothly, very much the director. 'To you and Paul. Happy days.' He raised his glass.

'Thank you.' She suspected him of undisguised mockery—there had been a wry twist to his mouth as he toasted her.

'Delightful party,' he added.

Now she was sure. He was mouthing platitudes, in some sort of hidden joke at her expense. All right. Two could play at that game. 'Not at all,' she assured him with vapid charm. 'My pleasure.'

He rose abruptly to his feet. 'I'm off,' he announced in much more familiar tones, as though it were the end of the ward round.

And just as if it had been, Gabrielle supposed the least she could do would be to see him out, and she turned to follow him. However, Andrew forestalled her. He, too, had shot to his feet, and he went after Robert as though catapulted. 'I wonder if I might come along?' he asked. 'I should so much value the opportunity to observe . . .'

They disappeared through the French windows, and Paul galloped after them, throwing back over his shoulder the hardly encouraging remark that he might be back or he might not, and not to worry.

Gabrielle sank into one of the empty chairs, and looked across at Nicola.

'Typical,' Nicola said. 'That's the last we'll see of any of *them*, if you ask me. Thank God I'm retired. I have no intention of rushing off to the ward to brood over this unfortunate child, fascinating though I'm sure she is. Shall we stay here and finish off the quiche? Or do you feel you have to go in and play hostess?'

'People can come and find me.' Gabrielle was crisp. 'If they want me.' Suddenly her engagement party had gone sour on her. She had had more than enough of the human race, in any of its forms.

CHAPTER TWO

AT TWO in the morning, Gabrielle packed a protest-ing Nicola and Andrew off home. Nicola's plan was for them to stay on and wash up, but Gabrielle firmly vetoed it. After they'd gone, she went straight to bed. She was off for the weekend, so she'd be able to have a lie-in and clear up the party debris comfortably in the morning.

The telephone broke into her sleep. Hazily, she consulted her bedside alarm. Seven o'clock. At this hour, it could only be the ward. 'Dr Vereker,' she announced sleepily, already resigned to the inevitable.

'Dr Scorer would like to see you in the ward as soon as you can make it,' the night staff nurse told her apologetically.

'On my way.' Gabrielle put the telephone down and swung her legs out of bed, scowling. So much for her lie-in. So much for her weekend off. Bloody man.

He was waiting for her in sister's office. 'Sorry to bring you over so early.'

He didn't sound in the least sorry, Gabrielle thought. 'I wanted to have a word with you about that patient we admitted last night. Thing is, I'm just off to Bramley House for my clinic. Paul's coming down with me, and I've sent Chris to bed

24

—told him not to surface before ten—he's been up most of the night. So that leaves you to cope with this child, I'm afraid. In any case, I'd be glad if you'd keep in touch and support Chris in his management once he comes back on.'

'Of course.'

'You'll remember what we were saying last night about this admission—well, we had a dicey time with the kid, and although she does seem over the worst, I'm still not entirely easy in my mind. She's not straightforward, by any means, and I'm not confident she'll settle now, in spite of appearances. I want you to keep the ventilator at the bedside, in case you need it—don't let anyone swipe it for some other patient—explain that to sister when she comes on. And the child must never be left out of sight. Tell sister that, too. I want a good nurse to see every breath this child takes, until you are sure it's no longer necessary. Right?'

'Yes, certainly.'

'Now let's go along and have a look at her.'

There was a nurse by the bedside, who rose as they entered and came to meet them at the door. 'She's dropped off,' she murmured.

'Good. Her colour's better,' Robert said in an undertone, and turned to Gabrielle again. 'Doesn't look too bad, considering, does she? But if you'd seen her last night, you'd have been worried.' He shook his head. 'Trouble is, if she relapses, after what she's already been through, she could very quickly become exhausted, and then she might need help with her breathing. I had intended to examine her with you before I leave, so that we could decide on management together, in the light of her present condition. More important for her to rest, though—so we won't disturb her. Thank you, Nurse.'

Gabrielle followed him out of the little cubicle and out to the landing, where he stopped. 'I've already written her up for everything I think she might need,' he told her. 'But you must use your discretion about when, and how much. Two main issues I want you to watch. One. Monitor the heart. Later on this morning, you might get one of the cardiologists along to check her over.'

'I'll do that.'

'Two. Make sure there's no underlying chest infection. I don't think there is, I think it was either allergy or some sort of emotional upset that triggered the attack, but we need to be sure, so get the bacteriology done. Then we need to know a great deal more about her present condition after this severe bout of asthma, so I want everything checked—blood alkali levels, respiratory function, and so on. As far as investigations are concerned, some people would throw the book at her. But there's the rub. Because—' he broke off. 'Because what? You tell me.'

Evidently the occasion was now switched into a teaching session. Luckily Gabrielle knew exactly what her chief was driving at—in fact, it had been difficult for her not to interrupt him to point out this particular snag. 'Because we don't want to tire her when she's already exhausted, nor do we at any price want her tensed up and moving straight into another attack.'

'Correct. So you'll need to adjust your investigations to her temperament. Calmness is all. That's one reason why I want you to hold Chris's hand. He'll need support in what not to do, as much as anything. When in doubt, sit back and wait.'

'I'll remember.'

'Melanie, her name is. Game little soul, and she had a very nasty struggle for breath all night through, and she does panic easily. So do try to be reassuring, and go very gently, won't you?' He eyed her dubiously.

Gabrielle was offended. He'd made his point once. He didn't have to reiterate it. What did he suppose her usual way with children to be, blast him? Militant?

As it turned out, he was not thinking about her. 'Try not to let Mum upset her,' he said. 'Dad's OK, but Mum's a very tense lady.'

'You want me to keep them apart?'

'Within reason. Do what you can. Right. Over to you. I'll be in touch after my clinic.' He nodded dismissal, turned on his heel, and was gone.

So much for her quiet morning.

She went back to the little cubicle, and looked down at the sleeping Melanie in the oxygen tent. A pretty child, but pale and thin, with tumbled dark curls over a high forehead. She seemed touchingly vulnerable, and Gabrielle experienced a sudden uprush of emotion, coupled with a driving determination. This frail child had been left in her

care, and she'd see her safely through, if she had
to stay here all day.

The sensation was familiar to her. Almost any
sick child could produce it. This, in fact, was how
her working day normally took her. She loved, if
not every minute—only a masochistic saint could
go as far as that—at least most hours of the twenty-
four, and how she was going to be able to bear to
leave these wards and this hospital for general
practice in Ledford or anywhere else she could not
conceive.

Hastily she pushed the disturbing thought away,
and turned back to the problem Robert Scorer had
left her.

Punctually at ten o'clock a bug-eyed Chris joined
her, exclaiming at once that the patient looked
immensely better than when he'd gone off at five
a.m.

Together they embarked on a battery of tests.
Awake, Melanie was not easy to handle. Tired and
tearful, she wanted only to be left alone with her
father, and turned away almost petulantly from all
the strange doctors and nurses who kept asking
her to do this and that for them. However, her
father, a burly slow-spoken man, turned out to be
a tower of strength. Plainly Melanie adored him,
and would do her best to carry out whatever he
asked. Her mother, Gabrielle was relieved to hear,
had gone home to get some sleep.

At twelve-thirty, when Robert Scorer rang from
Bramley House, she was able to tell him the patient
was much improved and they had achieved a good

deal of their programme. 'Her pulse charts have steadied, and the respiration rate has improved—Chris says she's quite different from when he was with her during the night.'

'Have you been on to the heart people about her?'

'Yes. The senior registrar was in, so I got him to come in and go over her. I told him she'd had a severe and rather prolonged attack, and that we were anxious about cardio-vascular over-burdening.'

'What did he say?'

'More or less gave her a clean bill. I'd done an ECG for him before he arrived, but he hardly glanced at it. He spent a long time on his physical examination, though, and found no evidence of any heart disease, either congenital or acquired.'

'Excellent. That's one problem off our backs, then. What about the bacteriology? Any evidence of respiratory tract infection?'

'No. Two smears negative, praise be.' Gabrielle knew better than to try to tell him how difficult it had been to take the smears. Consultants never wanted to be bothered with that sort of detail. In fact, Melanie had jibbed at having so much as a spatula on her tongue, let alone a swab down her throat, and had started to cry noisily. Her father, though, had come to the rescue. He'd talked cheerfully, ordered her to stop crying, which she'd promptly done, and then held her head while the procedure was carried out.

'FEV_1?' Robert was demanding.

This, the forced expiration volume taken over one second, a method of measuring the lung function, was not as high as it should have been, but on the other hand by no means as low as Gabrielle had been expecting.

Robert agreed with her. 'It all seems satisfactory. I don't think I need come back to London because of her, so I'll stay here and do my ward round as usual. Actually, it sounds as though Chris will be perfectly all right on his own now. Make sure he has your telephone number, though, won't you?'

'I will.'

'Right.' The telephone clicked off, and Gabrielle stared at it resentfully. Not one word of thanks or appreciation. He took her efforts entirely for granted.

Well, she reminded herself fairly, that after all was what she was paid for. She sighed, found Chris and had a quick lunch with him—during which they discussed Melanie non-stop—and then returned to the ward with him for another batch of respiratory function tests. It was mid-afternoon before she was able to return to her flat.

Here, of course, she was confronted by the debris of her party, looking extraordinarily unattractive and sordid. She stared round, disgusted. She'd forgotten all about last night's entertaining, and she was unimaginably tired. Happiness would be to stretch out on her big sofa and forget the world.

No way. She shot into the kitchen, brewed herself a strong black coffee, turned on the hot tap, tipped detergent into the sink, and began washing up.

After this she rang Chris, who informed her that Melanie was doing fine, sitting up and enjoying her supper. 'Looking very smart in a frilly nightie her mother's brought in, and really quite pleased with herself, basking in all the attention and beginning to show off like mad. Kids are amazing, aren't they?'

Gabrielle agreed fervently, and put the telephone down thankfully. A free evening, at least. She and Paul usually went out on Saturday evenings for a meal, sometimes a play, too. She was searching the evening paper to see what was on when Paul rang.

He was still down at Bramley House. What was more, he proposed to remain there.

Gabrielle could hardly believe her ears. First of all, last night, he missed the party. Now tonight, when they invariably had a date. No Paul. Robert Scorer, it seemed, was taking him to dinner. Gabrielle tried not to grind her teeth with temper. Bloody Robert Scorer, for ever muddling up her life.

'It was most interesting doing the clinic and then the ward round here. Fascinating. Tremendously useful experience,' Paul told her enthusiastically —evidently he'd missed the tooth-grinding at her end. 'Anyway,' he continued, brimming with good cheer, 'You'll be glad of a quiet evening, I'm sure. You can have an early night. You must be exhausted after the party.'

So he did remember there'd been a party. That was something, she supposed. 'I'll see you in the morning, then.' She put the telephone down. That was that. Her time was her own at last. She should have been delighted. Instead the flat seemed empty and sad, and she felt bereft.

She ought to get down to some work for the approaching examination for the Membership of the Royal College of Physicians, less than a month away. Some revision and an early night was exactly what she needed. Anyway, it was what she was going to get, and she had better lump it. Tomorrow was another day.

Tomorrow, when it arrived, failed to restore her morale—rather the opposite. To begin with, driving up to Ledford, she and Paul argued all the way. About Robert Scorer.

Paul regarded his chief as God's gift to an up-and-coming young registrar whose next appointment would be in general practice. 'I am so lucky to have had my first year with Sir Frederick, so eminent, such an able clinician, and then land Scorer for the second year. Stimulating. Challenging. And what a diagnostician. To work with him daily is fantastic experience.'

If only, Gabrielle realised later, she had kept her mouth shut at that point, they would not have spent the entire journey in heated disagreement. Fatally, though, she commented bitterly that it was a pity Robert Scorer, however brilliant he happened to be, was so inconsiderate. 'I know he never grudges the hours he spends in the wards himself. But he might occasionally think of his staff as well as the patients. I think the way he kept you in the ward on Friday evening, when he knew perfectly well it was our party, was the end. He was more than capable of seeing to the patient with Chris. He could have let you go off.' Gabrielle knew she was being unfair. She wouldn't herself have dreamt of turning her back on the director— in the person of Uncle Fred, say—in the ward with a critically ill child. But some compulsion to attack Robert Scorer had her in its grip, and she was determined to hold him personally responsible for what she was equally determined to regard as the failure of her party—which in fact she'd been assured by everyone had been an enormous success regardless of the absence of one of the principals.

'Of course I couldn't have cleared off,' Paul said. 'What on earth's got into you? Out of the question. What's more, if it hadn't been for him I wouldn't have shown up at all—it was his idea to come across, not mine.'

'His idea?' Gabrielle was shattered.

'That's right. "Can't leave Dr Vereker to hold the fort on her own," he said. "Nothing more we can do here for twenty minutes. Chris will do very nicely without us. Be a relief to him, I daresay."'

'What did Chris say to that?' Gabrielle was intrigued.

'Oh, he was all right. He knows how to deal with the director. He simply said "Not at all, sir. But I dare say I shall manage," and went on putting in the slow adrenalin. So off we went to the party—without him I would never have made it.'

Defeated on one front, Gabrielle switched to another. 'What about yesterday, then?' she demanded. 'Taking you down to Bramley House all day. Thoroughly inconsiderate and absolutely typical.'

'But Gaby, I asked him to take me.'

Gabrielle was deflated. 'You *asked* him?'

'Sure. I knew it would be interesting, and it was. The cases there were quite different from those we ordinarily see in the wards, for one thing. And the whole atmosphere is different, too. More relaxed. Homely, almost. After all, Gaby, I've only another three months to go as his registrar, and anything extra I can pick up along the way is invaluable. This first-hand experience of children in residential care was most worthwhile. And then he was kind enough to invite me to have dinner with him. We went to an extremely nice place he knew in the country nearby, had very good meal, and we were able to go over all the patients we'd seen in much more detail than there is normally time for. I am most grateful to him for allowing me to spend the day with him.'

They were still arguing about Robert Scorer and Bramley House when they arrived in Ledford and drew up outside the home and surgery of Paul's uncle and aunt, and at once Gabrielle found herself plunged into a new environment and new problems.

It wasn't that Viswanathan and Debi Singh were

not friendly and welcoming. Two small, cheerful and somewhat rotund people—Paul was a foot taller than his uncle—they invited Gabrielle into their home and looked after her in the kindest possible manner. But there was no mistaking the penetrating scrutiny they subjected her to, as well. They were tactful about it, didn't put her through any sort of catechism, but she was as much under assessment as if she'd already been up before the Membership examiners in the Royal College.

Gabrielle was reasonably certain she passed their tests. They seemed to warm to her, and to be ready to accept her as part of the family in future. It had been something of a surprise, though, to find there was any doubt about this. Until now, Gabrielle had imagined they'd be glad to find Paul intending to marry another doctor from his teaching hospital. This, of course, was what he'd assured her, and she had never questioned it. She should have known better. She was simply a strange English girl for whom Paul was preparing to renounce his commitment to the fiancée chosen by his parents. A serious step, as they pointed out.

Paul had told her the arrangement was to be cancelled, and that would be the end of that. She had accepted what he said unsuspectingly.

How wrong she'd been. As Robert Scorer— must he always be right?—had warned her.

Paul's uncle brought the problem out into the open. 'You have written, of course, to your parents, to tell them the exact situation?'

Paul had flinched, Gabrielle had seen it for herself. Her first real intimation of trouble. 'Not yet,' he admitted. 'To Anik, yes. But not to my parents so far.'

This was news to Gabrielle, who had been under the impression he had written both to his parents and to his fiancée by the same mail.

He cast her an appealing glance. 'When I came to write,' he explained uncomfortably, 'I felt it was only fair to Anik to give her a little warning. A chance to collect her thoughts, prepare herself, before my parents and hers knew about it.' He went on explaining to an unresponsive uncle and aunt that he and Anik would then be able to present a united front. They would be able to maintain, jointly, that they were in total agreement that the marriage should not take place.

Paul's uncle was forceful. 'You would have done much better to have told your parents before saying anything to Anik. They could have dealt with her and her family.'

'Oh, I couldn't have done that.' Paul shook his head. His eyes were unhappy, and held something else, too. Almost a look of tenderness, Gabrielle saw. A look she had imagined was only there for her. Now, though, it was for Anik. Startled, she began from that moment to understand that Paul's feelings for Anik were not, as he had asserted so often, non-existent. He remained protective towards her.

Protectiveness, of course, was his outstanding quality. He had been drawn by it into his speciality, child health. He would, everyone agreed, be a wonderful family doctor. He loved looking after people.

That, after all, was how they had come together. He had looked after her so gently and kindly during the first few agonising weeks of her first house job. She had been Uncle Fred's new, raw house physician, and Paul had been her registrar. Patient and caring, he had rescued her from any gaffes, whenever she called him. His protectiveness had warmed her and given her confidence—and had made her turn to him increasingly. Of course this same caring protection would be there for Anik. She should have expected it.

Uncle and nephew were now involved in vehement argument about the necessity for Paul to write immediately to his parents, and Paul's aunt turned to Gabrielle. 'It is so sad,' she said. 'Poor Anik. But we were afraid, my husband and I, that this arranged marriage would never come off. We warned Paul's father that he should not commit Paul in this way. Unfortunately, though, you see, Anik is daughter of very old friend of his. They have not prospered—in fact, they are hard up, and as a result they are without influence. At home, you know, in India, this is still important. To help his old friend, Paul's father promised this marriage for Anik. Otherwise, with no dowry, or none worth mentioning, Anik could not make suitable marriage.' Debi Singh pondered, her eyes sad. 'In my generation, you see, it would have worked, such arrangement. But Paul's parents send him to UK to medical school for all these years, and then expect him to marry girl of their choice as if he had never left.' She sighed. 'Indeed it is very sad for poor Anik, especially as she has been training as nurse to prepare herself for this marriage.'

Gabrielle was horrified. Paul had said nothing of this. Debi Singh was continuing. 'It is essential Paul writes immediately to his parents. Stat, as we would say in hospital, eh? Until he does so, until his parents know, our two families are having to consider Paul and Anik as bound to one another. You see?'

Gabrielle saw only too well. She nodded.

'So you must if necessary stand over him while he writes. Men are very good at putting off difficult actions.'

'But I can't possibly interfere. I never intended to step between him and Anik. I never will. If it is to be done, it must be his own doing. I'm not trying, I never have, to take him away from her. He told me that no matter what was to happen between him and me, he would never marry Anik.'

'I am sure, my dear, that you didn't try to influence him—except by existing, of course—but now that he has made his decision, I think you must step in and help him to carry it out. He is going to find it difficult to do. Paul never likes hurting people, and he is going to have to hurt Anik.'

Gabrielle protested. 'But he told me she'd be as glad to escape from the arranged marriage as he was.'

'Oh no.' Debi Singh was decisive. 'He is wrong there. But men don't understand these things. Poor Anik, this marriage is very likely her one and only chance to marry well and come to UK as doctor's wife. It is going to be very hard for her to learn it is all off. However, we must hope that her father may be able to find someone else suitable.'

Obviously, though, Gabrielle could see clearly, Paul's aunt had no belief in this convenient solution.

CHAPTER THREE

LATE ON Monday evening, surrounded by text-books, Gabrielle was sitting at her desk. She and Paul had agreed that with only three weeks to go before the examination, everything had to take second place to her work for the Membership.

'I shall leave you in peace,' he had said, on their return from the worrying visit to Ledford. 'I must deal with my own problems, and leave you to concentrate on the exam. That is most important thing just now. I might come in occasionally and give you quick *viva*, eh? Apart from that, we should not meet.'

A dreary programme, it seemed to Gabrielle, though she knew he meant well. It was just that all their recent dealings left her on edge. When she looked back to their early days, it seemed like a memory from another world.

The door bell rang. She was delighted. Paul had decided after all to look in on her. He had missed her, he was unable to stick to his self-imposed regime.

It was Paul right enough. With a long face and an air mail letter. A letter from Anik, he told her glumly. 'Everything I said she has misunderstood,' he began, before even stepping into the hall. He neglected, too, to kiss Gabrielle. Simply started talking. 'She is telling me how she has been fitting herself for our marriage and her move to UK, and how it is too late to change now. She only took up nursing, she say, to prepare herself for our marriage.' He was angry, even affronted, Gabrielle realised, as though Anik had deliberately set out to thwart him. Yet all she seemed to have been doing, Gabrielle saw reluctantly, was preparing realistically for a marriage she had presumably believed in. A cold wind of fear blew round the corners of Gabrielle's mind, but she pushed the fears away hastily, tried to reassure herself. Only a letter. No panic.

'Let me see the letter.' She hated reading it, yet she knew she must. None of this trouble need have arisen if only she had read Paul's letter to Anik in the first place. He'd offered it to her, saying he'd be glad of her advice, but she'd pushed it away, refused to look at it. To read his letter breaking off his engagement to another girl had struck her as a horrifying invasion of privacy. She had wanted nothing to do with it. She should have steeled herself, though, and read it carefully, using her head. If only she had done so, she would have noticed, surely, that it left room for doubt. She could guess what had happened. Paul had tried too hard to be kind, and as a result had failed to make himself plain. Reluctantly she began to read Anik's words.

'I have been preparing for our marriage ever since I left school. As you know, I entered the hospital here—your father's hospital—as a student nurse three years ago. I have taken my finals, and if I pass, which I'm sure I shall, I shall be registered nurse next month. Our matron is Central-trained, and I have already been accepted for postgraduate year as staff nurse at Central'—

'*Here*? She's coming *here*?' Gabrielle was appalled.

'So she says.' Paul shook his head. 'I knew none of this, or I would certainly have told you. I am amazed. But I suppose—I suppose, you know, they must have told me, in letters from home.' He frowned. 'My mother, she tells me so many things, so much, so many details about people I don't any longer even know what they look like, that I—well, I skip a lot. Nearly always. I mean to go back and read it again slowly, when I have time, but you know how it is, there's so much happening every day, the next letter comes before I've re-read the one before. My mother is always telling me I've forgotten things she's already informed me about.'

Gabrielle believed him. 'I can imagine. It must seem so shadowy compared with life here.'

'I ought to have checked on all this, though, before I asked you to marry me.'

True, of course. But not a solution. Gabrielle turned back to the letter. 'What else does she say? Um—yes. Here we are.'

'. . . . staff nurse at Central. This too has been your father's urging. As for my knowledge of English ways, which you say is worrying you, in order not to be encumbrance, I have asked English girl on staff to give me reading list of modern English novels, which she say will prepare me for what is like today.'

'Heaven help her,' Gabrielle commented, with a brief glint of humour. 'Honestly, Paul, she's doing very well. Being very sensible.' Against her will, the letter had touched her. 'In order not to be encumbrance,' Anik had written, and the clumsy but so obviously genuine fear had brought Anik to life, turned her into a person struggling against unforeseen disaster.

'She can't come here.' Paul sounded angry but looked, suddenly, terrified. 'I won't have it.'

'No, of course not.' Gabrielle spoke without conviction.

'But what can I say to make her understand?'

He sounded frustrated and irritable when Gabrielle was longing for sympathy and reassurance. However, what he needed was useful advice. She pulled herself together. 'I think,' she said slowly, 'that your uncle is right. You must tell your parents you want to marry me, and to call off your marriage to Anik. The sooner they know the better.' She hated saying this, it seemed so unkind to Anik. Yet what else could she say?

Paul accepted it. 'It's what I should have done in first place.' He sighed, and ran his hands through his thick dark hair. 'It's so difficult.' He knew exactly why he had not written first of all to his parents. Contrary to what his uncle suspected, fear of their disapproval had not held him back. He could deal with them. He had been standing on his own feet for eight years. In the beginning it had been hard, but he had achieved independence. It had been solely for Anik's sake that he had wanted to send a private warning before breaking the news to his parents. His aunt had been mistaken. Paul knew perfectly well what he was doing to Anik by ending their engagement. He knew what it was going to mean to her to remain in India, the arranged marriage fallen through, and he had hesitated for months before taking his decision. He had fought against his love for Gabrielle, had tried hard to turn his back on it, to remember only his duty to Anik. But his love for Gabrielle had been too strong, and then, finally, he had recognised that whether or not he was able to marry Gabrielle, he could not spend his life married to Anik. It would be fair to neither of them. He had tried, though, to be understanding when he wrote to her.

'I was a fool,' he said. 'I should have been more tough with her. Made her see I meant it. Would have been kinder in long run. That's what Scorer was pointing out to me, and he was right. Clean cut is best.'

Gabrielle was startled. 'Robert Scorer? Were you talking to him about Anik? And *me*?'

'No, no, of course not. It was about a child's parents, and what to tell them. But he said I am too apt to hesitate, imagining I am being kind, but that when bad news has to be broken it is no kindness to let yourself be misunderstood. You see? He might have been talking about Anik. Is same thing. He said parents of probably dying child only suspect that truth is being concealed from them, and they become demoralised or suspicious, especially if they see their small child slipping backwards when according to me he ought to be improving. Be reassuring and supportive *after* you've handed out unwelcome truth, he told me. I argued with him, because I think myself bad news ought to be told gradually, allowing people to take their time, come to terms with it at own pace. I see now though he may be right. Is no kindness to dither about.' He sighed. 'Certainly I ought to have been blunt with Anik, not let her assume I am anxious only about how she will adapt to UK And now I am in a spot.'

'We're both in a spot,' Gabrielle agreed, smiling ruefully. It seemed a ridiculously mild way of putting it.

'You are not,' Paul said at once. 'You are not involved in my stupid muddle. This affects you not at all. You stand where you have always stood. You are my love, and you will be my wife.' He took her face between his sure hands, his hands that she loved, that she had first watched for their gift of bringing calm to a frightened child. Like the children, she felt better immediately. 'This misunderstanding with Anik is sad for her and difficult for me, but it is nothing to you. Be sure of that. I shall extricate myself. I only, we are agreed, have to be a bit more tough, eh? I shall break unwelcome truth to Anik so that there is no misunderstanding. I shall tell her I do not intend to marry her, never mind reasons, never mind nursing training, marriage is off. Marriage is not for me and Anik. Is for you and me. No one else. So do not fear.' He smoothed her hair back with

gentle cherishing hands, and then held her to his
sturdy body and kissed her, slowly, lovingly.

With his arms round her and his mouth on hers
Gabrielle felt safe and warmed. Her cold anxiety
dissolved, and she leant against him and was sure
that nothing in the world could ever come between
them. Security was this. To be held in Paul's arms
for ever.

He was the one who ended it. 'I must not stay
here like this. You were revising, you were at your
desk, I can see it, and I come bursting in with
Anik's letter and interrupt you. You must go back
to your books, and I will go and write to Anik.'
He kissed her again, but briefly, like a husband of
many years off to catch the 8.45 as usual. More of
a peck than a kiss. He patted her kindly, if a
shade absent-mindedly—perhaps he was already
composing his letter, she thought—and walked
away down the passage. Her front door shut behind
him, with a final thud.

Gabrielle turned dutifully back to her desk, and
reread the paragraph in the chapter on intrinsic
and extrinsic asthma she'd been studying when he
arrived. It was not an easy passage at the best of
times, and now it seemed to have lost all meaning.
She frowned and reread it, but it failed to sink
in. Instead the phrases from Anik's letter spun
through her mind.

She ought not to have allowed Paul to go off
and answer it himself. They should have sat down
together and written the reply. A firm and unmistakable reply, that faced Anik with the unwelcome

truth, brought her to full realisation of the fact that there was going to be no marriage to Paul, no life in England for her.

Poor Anik. Poor unhappy Anik, training for three years as a nurse, simply to be ready for her marriage to Paul in England.

And now, instead of despairing for herself, Gabrielle began to despair for Anik in far-off India. What had they done to her, she and Paul?

Destroyed her.

Gabrielle felt as though she had intruded into some existing marriage, stolen away a hitherto loyal husband. Taken what she wanted, without counting the cost to anyone else.

No. This was not true. She pushed the guilt and pain away. She had done nothing to be ashamed of, and nor had Paul. He had tried hard to pretend, for months he had tried to pretend that what was between him and Gabrielle was not love, was no more than the casual friendship of two working partners.

She tried to still the rising desperation crowding her mind. She had entered into this engagement with Paul and she would be doing no service to anyone if she backed out. She would merely have transferred Anik's unhappiness to Paul. And to herself.

But what was she going to do?

She shook her head. She hadn't the faintest idea. Look where she might, there were no solutions.

The next morning, hardly surprisingly, she was heavy-eyed and pale, after a sleepless, anxiety-ridden night of worry. It was the teaching round. She knew she looked a wreck. Even so, she was put out when Robert Scorer's eye, passing routinely along the massed cohorts of his assembled staff—senior registrar, registrars, senior house officers, house physicians, pathologists, physiotherapists, social worker, a gaggle of students, and no less than three nursing officers—paused on her. He scanned her bleakly, and abruptly demanded, 'You all right, Dr Vereker?'

'Quite all right, thank you, sir.'

'Don't look it.'

She glared ungratefully back at him.

He chose to ignore her obvious ill temper. 'Sure you want to do the round? Go off if you like. Dr Lyall can take your cases for you.'

'Of course I can do the round.' She was affronted. 'There's nothing wrong with me. I just didn't sleep very well, that's all.'

Paul, standing at the director's shoulder, looked agonised, whether at her state of health or her rudeness to the director Gabrielle had no idea—nor, at the precise moment, did she very much care.

The round set off and trailed its way from bed to bed, into each side-room, across the landing and through the length and breadth of the other half of the ward, and finally back to the broad landing.

It had ended without her own actual disgrace, Gabrielle realised thankfully. She had not fallen down on the presentation of her own cases, she'd been adequate to the occasion. But only just. In no way could she have been said to have been a ball of fire and an ornament to the unit. In fact, visitors from other hospitals probably thought her a dead loss. A passenger.

As they were dispersing, the familiar clipped abrupt voice cut across the mutter of conversation like a knife. 'Dr Vereker.'

Gabrielle stopped in her tracks.

'One minute, if you wouldn't mind.'

He was going to tick her off, tell her she'd let them down, that she had to do better than that if she wanted to stay on his unit. It was well known that Robert Scorer refused to suffer fools gladly. If only her head wasn't pounding like a road drill. She followed him along the passage and into his office.

'Shut the door.'

Ominous. The door of the director's room stood open to all comers, unless he was interviewing new staff or breaking bad news to a patient's relative. Or, for a change, tearing Dr Gabrielle Vereker off a strip. Justifiably, too, she had to admit it to herself. His next words, though, took her by surprise.

'Sunday's visit to the Singh family not a success?'

How in the world did he know?

Of course, Paul must have told him when he explained about being out of reach all day.

'It—it was all right. It's just that—that I suppose I was tired, but I tried to do some revision as well when I got back, and I went on rather late, and then I couldn't sleep.' It sounded extraordinarily feeble, and for a mad moment she longed to tell him the whole story. But Robert Scorer was not

Uncle Fred, she reminded herself severely. In any case her problems were her own affair. Hers and Paul's. Idiotic to have this overwhelming urge to share them with her chief. As if he could alter anything.

His dark eyes, and to her astonishment they seemed sympathetic, searched hers. 'What have you got on this afternoon?'

'This afternoon?' she repeated, dazed.

'Two to six pm say,' he explained with unimpaired patience. 'After lunch.'

'Sorry. Um—I have . . .' Hastily she reeled off a string of that afternoon's chores.

'Leave them with me.'

'Ergh?' An unlovely sound. 'I mean, I'm sorry, but what exactly—'

'Leave them with me. I'll see to it they're done. You go off back to that flat of yours, have hot milk and aspirin, and go to bed. And sleep. See me here again—' he leafed through his diary 'yes, say at seven this evening. Right?'

'But I—but you—'

'No argument. Get lost. But no more revision, mind. Aspirin and bed. Right, girl. Out.'

Bemused, she followed his instruction.

'You look like death,' he threw after her, as she went through the door.

It only needed that.

In her flat she did as she'd been told. Heated milk, took aspirin, set her alarm for six o'clock, and went to bed. She refused to allow herself to dwell on any of her problems—not Anik, the Singh

family, the Membership approaching so inexor-
ably, not even the afternoon's work she'd aban-
doned. She slept until her alarm roused her. She
was rested, and her depression had lifted, so that
she had regained her confidence in herself and her
ability to cope. In future, she told herself, she'd
follow Uncle Fred's excellent advice. 'One thing
at a time,' he had often told her, when problems
came thick and fast. 'There's only one of you, you
can only handle each problem separately. So no
point in thinking about them all at once, either.
Achieves nothing, except to induce panic.'

All right. So what she had to think about now
was meeting the director at seven o'clock. Nothing
else. She ought to be keen and fit, ready for duty.

She showered, climbed into a clean shirt and a
newly pressed skirt, picked up her keys, her sling
bag and her notebook, grabbed her long-serving
black velvet jacket in case the evening air was
chilly, and walked briskly across to the unit and
Robert Scorer's office.

'Ha,' he said as she entered. 'Looking a good deal
better. Amazing what a few hours sleep can do.'

'Yes, you're right. It was very good of you to
make it possible.'

'What you need next is a square meal.'

She'd come over expecting to catch up on the
afternoon's work. 'Oughtn't it to—I mean, this
afternoon—'

'We'll discuss this afternoon over some food, shall
we? Care to join me for a meal at Giovanni's?'

'Oh, but are you sure—'

'Wouldn't ask you if I wasn't.'

'It's very good of you,' she said tritely. Any originality of thought or expression seemed to have deserted her. She hoped he didn't think her too drearily banal.

'Come on,' he said. He'd already shed his white coat—she saw it hanging on the door—and he reached for his jacket and shrugged himself into the formal navy pin stripe of a teaching hospital consultant, at once looking immensely senior and eminent. To her annoyance Gabrielle experienced a tremor of alarm at the prospect of eating a meal with him. Irritably she pushed her anxiety away. He wasn't going to examine her for the Membership here and now. She was perfectly presentable. They had her cases to talk about. Surely she could share an evening meal with her chief without suddenly being reduced to a quivering jelly? Where was her pride? Hastily dredging this truant quality up from within her, she followed him out of the office and along the corridor.

Giovanni's was an Italian restaurant near the Central much frequented by hospital staff. Over the years the restaurant had prospered, spreading first upstairs and then into the next-door shop. At the same time a clear distinction between upstairs and downstairs had emerged. Downstairs was for hungry juniors in a hurry, upstairs for consultants, senior registrars and the occasional celebration.

Robert Scorer led the way upstairs, they were wafted to a table in the window overlooking Great St Anne's, the main shopping street opposite the hospital, and Robert began ordering. 'May as well fill you up, now I've got you here,' he commented. 'How about starting with a nice plate of pasta?'

A nice plate of pasta would normally have constituted Gabrielle's main meal, but she was not going to say so to Robert Scorer. Not at any price. 'That would be great,' she said agreeably, as if three or four-course meals were her daily routine.

The pretty Italian waitress, once the pasta had been decided, inquired about wine.

'Please,' Robert said. 'Chianti. The Ruffino I had the other day.'

She handed him the wine list.

He scouted about in it, and pointed. 'No. 27.'

The waitress wrote it down, and departed.

Their pasta came, and a mound of cheese. Gabrielle stirred and mixed and ate. As always at Giovanni's it tasted very good, it was immensely filling, and she adored it.

The wine came, and was poured. Robert Scorer raised his glass to her.

Gabrielle was even more bemused than she'd been earlier. Was she actually sitting here, upstairs in Giovanni's, not only having a meal with her chief, the well-known woman-hater and spine-chilling chauvinist, but being toasted by him in a glass of Chianti? She was.

'Success in the Membership,' he said.

'Oh—er—yes. Thank you. I certainly hope so, but all the same—'

'All the same, you could try drinking to it,' he suggested, and suddenly his dark eyes were alive, not with contempt at all, but with an amused sort of friendliness. She found it both warming and—and what? Exciting? Surely not. 'Go on, be brave,' he said. 'Not superstitious, are you?'

'No, of course not.' She was indignant. A fine thing if he imagined her to be the sort of girl who scanned her horoscope in hopes of passing the Membership. 'The Membership,' she said, with some solemnity, and raised her glass.

They finished their pasta, and a second course of fillet of veal in an almost aromatic white sauce with tomatoes and courgettes—though in Giovanni's they had to be known as zucchini. Gabrielle found to her surprise she seemed to possess an enormous appetite, and she tucked in happily. When Robert Scorer tried her out on a series of tricky questions from previous Membership examinations she was almost pert with him, rapping out fast replies with gusto.

To her astonishment, the competence of her answers put him into another of his rages. 'And you're the candidate,' he exploded out of a clear sky, 'who's proposing to turn your back on the Central and go into general practice—interspersed with having babies and raising kids.'

She wasn't going to sit down under this. All right, so he had been amazingly kind and thoughtful today, but that didn't mean he had all the answers to everything.

'If you can tell me how a woman is to have a career and a family without sacrificing something along the way, I'd be delighted to hear it.'

'I know. I know it's difficult. But there are moments in a career when breaks can be taken without too much damage. You seem set on throwing everything away at precisely the wrong moment.'

'So you think I ought to turn my back on Paul, and get on with my career, trusting that when my own position is assured, some man who's as right for me as he is will miraculously surface at my side?'

Robert would have liked to say that that was exactly what he did mean. Almost any man would be less disastrous for Gabrielle than Paul Singh. However, even he knew this would be going too far. 'What I think you should do,' he said mildly, 'is to put Paul—and his difficulties over his former fiancée in India—right out of your head for the next three weeks. Concentrate solely on the Membership. Lock into that as if your life held nothing else—as it damn well shouldn't at this juncture. It may make a difference to your entire future, you realise that? Once you've got the Membership safely stashed away, you may, if you must, throw your career down any old drain. You could still pick it up years later, if you had to. Not that I'm at all in favour of your doing anything of the sort. I think, as I've said before, you should stay at the Central and do two years at least as a registrar.'

'I'll try,' Gabrielle promised. 'To carry out the first part of your advice, I mean,' she added hastily.

'It shouldn't be that hard. You can't have qualified in medicine without learning self-discipline.

There must have been other periods when you've had to turn your back on everything except work.'

This was true. She looked back into the past and remembered how it had been when her mother fell in love and married again, and took off for Canada for ever. Gabrielle had been shattered. She'd still been at school, and it had been the summer of her Q Levels. She had buckled to then, and managed to take the exams in her stride. During her grandmother's long illness, too, opportunity for study had been limited. There had been cooking and housework and caring for Gran, worrying about her, too. But she had somehow put every spare minute to good use, and qualified—though not, sadly, until after Gran's death. She had longed for Gran, a tower of strength throughout her life, to have seen her qualified and practising. Gran—the thought hit her like a blow—would have wanted her to take the Membership and be a registrar at the Central.

Darling Gran. Gabrielle had had to watch her dying, and she had known, because she had learnt enough to be certain about it, that Gran was not going to survive. The pain of her understanding had torn her apart.

It had not, however, prevented her from working. The memory jolted her.

'When my grandmother was dying,' she said, 'I went on working, I must admit. And in some ways to work, to lose myself in my subject for an hour or two, came as a relief.'

Robert nodded. 'It can often be quite an effort

to switch out of your own personal problems and into the needs of the wards,' he agreed. 'But once you've succeeded in doing it, you find it gives you a respite. When relaxation is unattainable, work can step in and take your mind off unbearable problems. Particularly when it happens to be work like ours, where human beings in pain are depending on you and you can't let them down. To give them half your attention or less is unthinkable— and this turns out to be as good for you as it is for them.'

Gabrielle nodded. 'That's true.' Robert Scorer, she suspected, had actually been telling her about his own experience during the break-up of his marriage. He'd said nothing to anyone about this, but everyone at the Central had the story at their fingertips.

'Often, when things go wrong personally,' he was saying, 'there's little you can do except allow time to pass. And there's nothing like work for filling up time. So get stuck into the Membership, will you, and put Paul into second place for a while. Quite possibly, by the time the Membership is behind you, you'll find that Paul has solved his problems too.'

'You may be right.'

'I hope I am.'

'So do I.' She smiled wryly. 'At any rate I'll follow your advice, and turn my back on everything except the Membership.'

CHAPTER FOUR

AFTER outpatients, as Paul was leaving for the ward, Robert called him back.

'Paul. One minute. A word with you. Shut the door. Now look here, I want to speak seriously to you about Dr Vereker.'

Paul was momentarily bewildered. 'About Gabrielle?'

'Exactly. We have the same individual in mind.' Robert was sarcastic. 'As far as I'm concerned,' he went on, with small regard for truth, 'your private affairs and your two fiancées are your own concern. But Dr Vereker's attempt at the Membership is a unit concern. I must ask you not to hold her back.'

'But—'

'Quite what you were both thinking of, getting engaged and throwing a party, of all things, just before the examination I shall never know. Even if you had been free to marry her.' A bleak eye surveyed Paul unkindly. 'However, what's done is done. But the Membership examination is ahead. Just over two weeks ahead, I may remind you. What I'm asking of you is that at least you don't hold her back. No interference with her studies, if you don't mind. If you can't help, try not to hinder. All right?'

Paul nodded unhappily. 'All I can say on my

own behalf is that I was under the impression everything would be straightforward. Of course, I should have made sure but—but, well, to be honest, sir, I just found myself proposing to her one evening.'

He looked miserable, and some of Robert's anger left him. 'I can understand how it happened,' he said, less curtly than before. 'In future, though, try to keep Dr Vereker's commitment to the Membership in the forefront of your mind.'

Paul promised fervently that he would do exactly that. 'I am hoping to be able to give her a little coaching,' he added. 'I may even be of some small use, perhaps.'

'Just don't muck things up, that's all I ask.'

Upstairs in Giovanni's at his regular table in the window later that day, Robert couldn't help remembering the evening when Gabrielle had sat opposite him. Well, he'd done what he could to help her. Now he should put them both, Gabrielle and Paul, out of his mind.

Instead, he sat there at his table, drinking Giovanni's excellent brew of strong coffee, and remembered his first introduction to Gabrielle on his arrival at the unit, three months earlier. It had been Uncle Fred who had pointed her out.

'That's the one to watch,' he'd said, 'that dark slip of a girl.' He'd nodded a little smugly. 'Been watching her myself, since she was a student—and not for the obvious reason either, I may say, though she's an astonishingly pretty girl. She was my house physician, you know, and I gave her a hard time.

Deliberately. I wanted to be sure she had the right stuff in her. She has.'

Robert had been surprised. He had even wondered if the old man, nearing retirement, had been taken in by the charm of having such a pretty girl constantly at his beck and call as his house physician, day in, day out, for six months.

Uncle Fred had read his scepticism unerringly. 'Not in my dotage, my boy. And don't you make the mistake of underrating her because she happens to be good-looking. She has brains and judgment. And she's going to the top. Mark my words.'

'The top, sir?' Robert didn't believe a word of it.

'That's right. Oh, I know—out of each intake of students we'll be lucky if more than one or two turn out to be high flyers. But Gabrielle Vereker is one of them. Keep an eye on her when I've gone, will you? Even if you are a doubting Thomas, look after her. She may need a bit of a helping hand— no family behind her. Had quite a hard time as a student. Lived with her grandmother, who died when Gabrielle was in her third or fourth year. So the girl has no one.'

Gabrielle had no one. Only Uncle Fred, and now himself. He wished he was better at handling staff. The only solution that so far occurred to him was to liquidate Paul Singh. Or instead, as an alternative, to shake Gabrielle until she came to her senses.

After his ward round the next day he asked her if she could do with any extra coaching. 'I could give you the odd hour here and there if it would be any help.'

Gabrielle glowed. The offer was unprecedented. In his abrupt, off-hand way, Robert Scorer was recognised to be a brilliant teacher and lecturer. To have his personal tuition in the run-up to the Membership would make her the envy of every other candidate. 'I'd be enormously grateful,' she told him.

'Right,' he said. He glanced at his watch, turned on his heel, and made off. From halfway down the corridor, though, he turned and threw a phrase back in her direction. 'Ring you later to fix a time.' He sketched a vague sort of salute, raising his pen to his brow, turned again, and she watched his lean white-coated figure disappearing round the corner.

Gabrielle went back to her own flat that evening in a cheerful frame of mind. She was going to put in a good evening's work on her books, and in a day or two, Robert might be there with her taking her through tricky bits of revision. He'd expect her to know her groundwork thoroughly, and she'd certainly not get away with being a mere passenger. She'd have to contribute her own insight—even flashes of diagnostic flair—or he'd feel he was wasting his time. But this was the kind of challenge she knew exactly how to meet, and the prospect gave her a sense of elation.

The door bell rang.

Paul stood there holding, ominously, another airmail letter.

Gabrielle's spirits collapsed.

'A follow-up letter from Anik,' he told her. 'She is begging me to say nothing to my parents until she is safely here in UK. She is fearing that if I say anything before she leaves she will never get to London at all. Her own parents will never consent to her coming here to train except as my fiancée, sponsored by my parents, and then by my uncle and aunt over here, she says.' He handed over the letter. 'Read it.'

'So please help me by saying nothing,' Gabrielle read. 'Afterwards, once I am established in London and working at the Central, we can tell both our parents. We can say we have found we do not suit, and neither of us is wanting the marriage. They will not like it, but it will be possible, once I am in UK, when it is too late for anything to be cancelled. I am qualified nurse, after all, and I will be able to manage quite well on my own at the hospital. All I am asking is that you tell no one before I reach London. After that I look after myself.'

Gabrielle experienced a wave of painful sympathy, and the thought that she herself might be the cause of the cancellation of Anik's year in London as a staff nurse upset her. With Anik's future at stake, her request to Paul for temporary silence didn't seem much to ask. 'I feel in some ways what Anik asks is the least you can do for her,' she said.

Paul nodded unhappily. 'It doesn't seem much to ask,' he agreed. 'The only thing is, suppose she was here, and she didn't keep her side of bargain?

What then? Suppose she tried to hold me to our marriage contract?'

'Then you'd have to say no.' Gabrielle was brisk, though her heart lurched wildly. 'It takes two to make a marriage, after all.' She sounded calm, but she didn't feel it. If Paul was unable to break off his engagement by letter, was he any more likely to be able to do it face-to-face with Anik?

'It's up to you,' he told her. 'That's why I brought you the letter to read. You have the right to decide. If you want me to, I'll ignore what she says, write to my parents now, today, and tell them everything.' He frowned. 'It's what I should have done in first place, I see that. But I'll do it tonight if you want me to. It isn't too late.'

'Oh, but it is,' Gabrielle said. Had it always been too late, she wondered? Nothing was changed, now, except that where before she had been ignorant, now she understood Anik's predicament and her feelings. 'Oh, Paul,' she said. 'It's such a muddle. I don't know what to say. But I don't see how we can let Anik down. It would be like basing our own future on her unhappiness. We can't do that.'

'Then I say nothing to anyone until she is here and doing her training?'

'I suppose that must be what I mean.'

He shook his head. 'That may be best for Anik, but it's very hard on you. All I've done is place her problems on your shoulders.'

It felt exactly like that, of course. But Gabrielle shrugged it off. 'We share our problems, don't we?' she asked. 'After all, if we are planning to share our lives, this is what it means. Sharing these difficulties.'

'That is what it is,' he said, relieved. 'You and I will tackle this together, eh?'

'Oh, Paul,' she began, and sighed. 'When you're here and we're together it seems so simple. We love each other, we belong together. What else is there? If only—'

'If only I could abandon Anik to whatever her future may be. That's what I should do. But I cannot. Simply I cannot do it.'

'It seems too brutal.'

'But I owe it to you to try. I ought to try.'

They spent another half-hour going round the problem, but reached no different conclusion.

'I must go,' Paul said. 'And leave you to your revision. I ought not to be interrupting you like this.' He kissed her gently. 'I'm so sorry I bring you nothing but trouble.' He took her into his arms and held her tightly. She could feel his heart beating against her breast, while his eyes searched her own. In their depths she read the love and tenderness that had always been there, that had offered so much comfort.

Tonight, though, she found no comfort there. She was facing the fact that Paul whom she valued because of his tenderness and compassion could because of these very qualities never willingly hurt Anik.

What, then, of their own future? Were there to be three of them always?

There was no doubt that Paul's commitment to Anik went much deeper than either he or she had guessed until it was put to the test. Ought she herself never to have accepted Paul in the first place, she asked herself? After all, she had known about the arranged marriage, he'd explained it to her.

Unaware of the lines her thoughts were taking, he kissed her again, and said 'I really must go, and give you a chance to work. I'm glad I came round, though. I feel so much better about everything now we've had a chance to talk it over.'

Gabrielle saw him out, shut the door on him, and returned to her desk. She wished she felt better for seeing him, but she felt much worse.

What was going to happen to them?

She did not dare to think. She sat down at her desk, and stared at her textbook, trying to lose herself in the intricacies of childhood asthma. But between her and the pages phrases from Anik's letter kept surfacing.

What was she going to do about her? Ought she to encourage Paul to forget their plans together and marry Anik?

Very nice for Anik, but hardly fair to Paul. He loved her, not Anik. All he was trying to do was to help a girl his parents had engaged him to formally in years long past. He was in fact being extraordinarily kind to Anik, when all he wanted was to be free. Many men, surely, would simply have informed their parents they were not prepared to go through with this out-of-date arrange-

ment, and left Anik to whatever her fate might be
without a second thought.

But then Paul was not like that. Paul was kind
and protective. That was one reason she had fallen
in love with him herself. So she owed it to him to
be the same. She must be understanding and
loving, and thrust right out of her mind the growing
suspicion that what she wanted was a way of
escape, a chance to get away, somehow, anyhow,
from this intolerable position as part of a triangle.

The next morning, after another sleepless night,
she was tense and edgy. Brushing her cloud of
dark hair before the mirror in her bedroom before
twisting it into its knot, she confronted a haggard
wreck, bags under her eyes and a colourless, almost
pasty skin, she thought. She took extra time to
make up her face, but the result was unimpressive,
and she went over to the wards knowing she looked
her worst.

When he came into the ward for a consultation,
Robert gave her one of his probing stares, and she
prayed fiercely that he wasn't going once again to
send her home to aspirin and hot milk. However,
he made no comment on her appearance, though
more than once she caught his eye on her. It
seemed, however, to hold irritation more than
concern, she was almost relieved to find.

She couldn't bear it if he was sorry for her.

The consultation over, he paused by the swing
doors on his way out. 'I could fit in an hour's
coaching this evening, if you like.' His eyes scruti-

nised her again, dubiously. 'Unless you're too tired.'

'No, of course I'm not too tired,' she said hotly. She was tempted to accept his offer, to throw Paul and his problems to one side, concentrate on work and her own personal success in her career. But she knew she couldn't, and reluctantly—with some embarrassment, too—she had to refuse. 'It's terribly kind of you, but I'm afraid I have to go out.'

His glance was cutting. 'Out? With the Membership two weeks away? Chancing your arm a bit, aren't you?'

This was what she felt herself, but Paul wanted her to go with him to Ledford for a family conference about Anik's latest letter. She would have liked to explain this to her chief, even to confide in him about the difficulties that had arisen. But he was already shouldering through the door, impatient to be on his way, so she said only that unfortunately the engagement was one she couldn't cancel.

He threw her a scathing glance, evidently visualising her living it up with Paul in a restaurant or disco all evening, and snapped, 'Up to you, after all, how you choose to spend your free time.' The doors swung behind him.

In the circumstances she was not altogether delighted, at the precise moment she was stepping into Paul's car, to see him come out of the main building.

In Ledford, the Singhs were pessimistic.

'I must tell you frankly,' Paul's uncle said. 'I

think if Anik once comes to UK, you will very likely end up having to marry her.'

Gabrielle went cold.

'How can you not?' Dr Singh was continuing. 'Once she is here, she is sponsored by us, by our family. Why? Because you are to marry her. It will be much more difficult to send her home unwed than to prevent her coming.'

'I should, just as you said, have written to my parents in the first place,' Paul agreed. 'But it seemed only kind to warn Anik first.'

'Yes, well, now you have warned her, and she is taking steps to protect herself, if you ask me. So you must act at once. Call it off publicly, write back to her firmly explaining that there can be no question, no question whatever, of coming to UK to join you—because that is what she is proposing, you know—and write to your parents at same time. Tell them about Gabrielle, too. Have you told Anik you are wishing to marry Gabrielle yet?'

'Not so far.'

'You must do so immediately. If you do not, and Anik arrives here, Debi and I will have to look after her, you see. We can do no other. She will be here under our protection.'

'And then we shall be split.' Mrs Singh spelled it out to Gabrielle. 'My dear, I am so dreadfully sorry. But if Anik comes to UK, to us, we shall have to try to see that her marriage to Paul is achieved. We can do nothing else. It will not be because we have changed towards you in any way. But there is this family commitment, and if Anik leaves her own home and comes to ours, we shall have no option but to honour it.'

Gabrielle felt as if she had been slapped in the face.

Paul gave her no chance to speak. 'This I cannot allow,' 1 e shouted furiously. Quietly-spoken, gentle Paul, who never never raised his voice in the wards, was strident. Carried away with anger, he banged the table. 'This cannot be. I cannot allow it. It is wrong. Wrong, do you hear? I am only trying to help Anik, to do my best for her. I am not going to marry her. I am going to marry Gabrielle. Take it or leave it, that is what I shall do.'

Everyone spoke at once, shouting each other down, interrupting one another. Only Gabrielle sat in unhappy silence.

'It's not Anik's fault,' Paul said. 'She herself has done nothing to jeopardise our marriage or to make it in any way unsuitable. I am the one who is defaulting, and I owe her any arrangements I can make to help her. I have to face fact. By not wanting marriage with her, I may be giving her worse life. Luckily times have changed. These days even Indian girl from good family can leave home and come to London to work and be independent. This is what I want to help Anik to do. That is what I owe her. I do not owe her marriage, whatever her father and mine may have decided years back. Anik, I am sure, understands this.'

'I would not be too certain about that,' his aunt warned him.

He paid no attention. 'To take this year's training here is good plan. Big step forward in her career, and I must help her to do it. Not stop her, humiliate her by telling my parents I no longer want to marry her. Just because at home in India they are living in last century is no reason why we should behave same way. Anik is my generation. I want to see she is all right, sure enough, but I do not want to marry her.' He turned to Gabrielle. 'So tell me. You have only to say, and I will do it. As I have said all along, if you want me to stop her coming, to do exactly as they advise,' he gestured at his uncle and aunt, 'write to my parents and tell them I am not going to marry Anik but you, then I will do it. You have only to say. It is your decision. I am in your hands.'

But Gabrielle, though she could see it would be wise, could not bring herself to do this to Anik. She owed Anik her chance, whatever came of it. To build her life with Paul on Anik's despair was unthinkable, and Gabrielle knew she could never do it. Neither she nor Paul. They were not made that way.

'No,' she said firmly and clearly. 'I don't ask that of you. I don't want you to stop Anik from coming here.'

'My dear,' Mrs Singh said, 'I respect your decision. But you are dreadfully mistaken. Hard it may seem—indeed, it *is* very hard—but Paul should tell his parents how matters stand, and stop Anik from coming.'

'Sometimes,' Dr Singh told her, 'it is necessary

to be wise in the ways of the world, and to steel oneself to do uncongenial act. You should do this now, I am telling you. Or there will be price to pay.'

Neither Paul nor Gabrielle would give in, and they returned to London tired and dispirited, no agreement reached. Paul dropped Gabrielle off at her flat, begging her not to worry.

'It may seem that there is no way ahead,' he told her. 'But I am sure there is. We shall win through in the end.'

'Yes, of course we shall,' she agreed.

A false front. Alone in her flat, she paced about, trying to face the future. If Anik came to London —no, *when* Anik came to London, then very likely she herself was going to lose Paul. Gabrielle could see it coming inevitably towards her, as night follows day.

Yet to sacrifice Anik in order to safeguard her own position—no. She could never do it. No matter how convenient they might be, some actions were unthinkable, and this was one of them.

If she and Paul were to be happy together, then Anik too must have her chance.

Gabrielle could see, though, that she might be risking everything. For if Anik came to London, the power of the family might be too strong for Paul.

CHAPTER FIVE

THE MEMBERSHIP examination was only four days away. The unit watched Gabrielle and forecast failure for her. Less than a month ago, they'd assumed the opening of a brilliant career would be signalled when she sailed through the Membership, gaining it at her first attempt and within two years of first qualifying in medicine. But now, they told one another bitterly, they could only give her less than a fifty-fifty chance.

'Fatal to involve herself with engagement parties and marriage plans with the Membership coming up,' they commented righteously.

'Such a pity, but just like a woman,' someone added, shrugging and raising tired eyes heavenwards.

'Is it true, do you know, that Paul Singh's fiancée in India has surfaced and is raising difficulties? Awkward, if so.'

'You can see why Gabrielle's looking more than a bit haunted recently. Do you think the marriage is off?'

'Should never have been on, if you ask me.' This from a well-known stickler for hard work, examination success and no private life before consultant status.

Over Gabrielle, though, most of them agreed

with him. 'She should have concentrated on the Membership.'

Their forecasts proved only too correct. Gabrielle fell at the first hurdle. Her paperwork let her down. Not enough revision, she thought despairingly. She knew she had not worked long enough or hard enough, while her inability to clear Anik out of her mind had played havoc with her memory.

Even so, to fall at the first hurdle like this shattered her. Until she failed, she hadn't guessed that somehow or other she had counted on passing. She had been expecting to be able to put the magic letters, MRCP, Member of the Royal College of Physicians, after her name for all to read. To have no right to do so still came as a nasty shock.

This was the first real failure in her career. At school, she had routinely won prizes and come top in examinations, transferring comfortably from junior school into the grammar school with a scholarship. O and A levels and entrance to the medical school at the Central followed, and even during her pre-clinical years she had been marked down by the dean as a strong candidate.

In fact, until Paul Singh came into her life she'd had it made, they said.

'To throw it all away like that simply because she's lost her head over one of our own registrars.' Bewildered and disappointed, the dean shook his head. 'I don't understand it—couldn't she have waited until she had the Membership safely behind her? What's all the hurry?'

Robert Scorer was furious. She'd let herself down,

and the reputation of his unit, too. What did the stupid girl mean by throwing her future away like this? Couldn't she have kept her emotions in check until after the examination? Bloody women. Unstable. Emotional. Never to be depended on.

And then, unexpectedly, he revolted against his own anger. Who was he to talk? He looked back to his own chaotic behaviour as his marriage crumbled, and knew that he too had been distracted and had risked his career, stumbled on what until then had been a highway to the top. He'd managed to pull himself together and retrieve lost ground, but it hadn't been easy.

All right. So that made two of them.

At least Gabrielle still had Paul around, to mop her up and condole with her. Robert supposed he should be glad of that. He wasn't. The recollection of Paul's part in her collapse renewed his rage, and it was in a vile temper that he made his way over to the King's Head. He wasn't in the mood for eating at Giovanni's tonight. He'd have a quick drink and a sandwich in the King's Head.

At a small table, chic in a tailored linen suit but with a face as long as a wet weekend, morosely nibbling a sausage on a stick, he discovered Gabrielle, receiving the condolences of most of the unit—but not, as far as he could see, of Paul.

He collected his beer and shouldered his way across to join them. 'Bad luck,' he told her briefly. 'Where's Paul?'

She turned strained eyes on him, and his heart jolted. The poor lost child.

Ridiculous idea. What had come over him? Just a silly girl on his staff who'd thrown her future away. Paul should see to her.

'I don't know where he is,' she was saying. Ashamed of her failure, her eyes avoided Robert's. 'I rang him, but I couldn't track him down. I thought perhaps I might find him here.'

'Paul, you mean?' One of the paediatric registrars from the professorial unit joined them. 'He's gone to Ledford, to see his uncle or something. Asked me to stand in for him.'

'Oh, that explains it,' Gabrielle said. 'I won't hang about any more for him.'

She looked desolate, and Robert was angrier than ever. What did Paul Singh suppose he was playing at? Why wasn't he around when he was needed? Surely he must have realised Gabrielle would need his support?

In the midst of this furious rage, Robert heard his own voice informing Gabrielle that he was taking her out for a meal.

She was alarmed. 'Oh, but—I mean—you don't have to. I shall be quite all right. I'm—I'm not—'

'Don't quibble, girl. Drink up and come along. I wasn't looking forward to eating on my own, anyway.' That was no more than the truth, after all. 'I'll have to call in at the flat first, to tell them where I'll be—I said I'd be at home for the rest of the evening. But if you wouldn't mind coming with me, I'll ring through, and we can book a table somewhere and be off.'

They walked out of the King's Head together, a

good many eyes following them. After they'd gone, a mild chorus broke out.

'What on earth can Paul be thinking of, not to be around when that poor girl has just failed the Membership?'

'All very well saying poor girl. We all know she's brought it on herself.'

'Perhaps. But it doesn't make it any easier to take, does it, when you know your failure can be laid at your own door?'

'I'm surprised at Robert Scorer, though. Now if it had been Uncle Fred—'

'If it had been Uncle Fred, he'd have seen to it that she passed the Membership.'

'How? Just tell me that.'

'He'd never have let this affair with Paul get so out of hand at just the wrong moment. He'd have managed to separate them—sent one of them packing. On some course, or to Bramley House. He was good at that sort of thing.'

'Can't expect Robert Scorer to turn into a father-figure like Uncle Fred overnight.'

Father-figure, though, was exactly how Robert cast himself as he took Gabrielle up in the lift to his sixth-floor flat in the new block round the corner from the hospital.

Even Gabrielle was momentarily diverted from her misery and felt a tremor of excited curiosity, as she ascended in the lift with her normally curt and monosyllabic chief, to spend the evening with him and to see, for the first time, his flat—about which there'd been considerable speculation in the unit.

What sort of mood would he be in? Had he brought her here to demolish her, reduce her to pulp? After all, he had warned her.

Inside the flat, she was surprised out of her worry. 'What a fantastic view.'

In his living room, a panorama of London confronted her through great floor-to-ceiling windows. Oddly enough, she had never expected Robert's flat to be spectacular. She had supposed he would live in some studious library-style apartment, floor-to-ceiling books ranged round the walls, certainly, but otherwise hardly different from Uncle Fred's London home, with its Persian rugs and antiques.

Nothing like that here.

'The views *are* nice,' he agreed. 'Otherwise the place has nothing going for it, I'm afraid. It looks what it is. Contract-furnished.'

'Contract-furnished?' She was puzzled. 'Can you do that?' This was a new idea. No one else in Gabrielle's world had done anything similar.

He saw he'd grabbed her attention, and since a break from examination blues was obviously a good plan, he set to and told her exactly what he'd done. 'Until now I've lived mainly in furnished places—hospital quarters or furnished tenancies—so I had nothing much to put here, except for my old desk. So I walked along the road to Heal's, to get some ideas.' He laughed abruptly.

'And?' She was intrigued.

'And I walked out again fast, I can tell you. I had no notion furniture cost those sort of prices.' It had been an illuminating experience, and for the first time he had faintly grasped what Lucilla had been driving at when she had so often accused him of not giving her the home she had a right to expect. 'I walked up the road and found myself outside Habitat. So I went in. I had to buy something to live here at all, even if no more than a bed, a chair and a table. Plus bookshelves. The books were here on the floor in toppling piles. So I took a look around, discovered they had a catalogue, took that away with me to study, and then rang up and ordered more or less half a dozen of everything, except for the table and the bed. I confined myself to one each of those to start with.'

'I like it.'

He shrugged. 'Practical and inoffensive. Looks more like a students' hostel than a home, if you ask me.'

'Oh no, not a bit. Full of light and air. Pale wood, and pale colours. Spacious and restful. It's great. This table, for instance—terrific.'

He laughed. 'I bought that because I thought it would be nice eventually in an old barn I've got in the country. It's even more bare than this flat. But the table is right for it, so I thought it would do here as a start, to eat off, and later when I find a proper dining table I like, it can go down to the barn.'

Gabrielle ran her hand slowly along the untreated pine of the big table, simple and plain as a table could be. Round it stood white metal chairs with natural canvas seats and backs.

'Director's chairs, they call these,' he explained. 'I bought them on the same principle. They'll trans-

fer to the barn and do out of doors—if I ever
get round to making a garden there—and in the
meantime they're most useful here.'

Gabrielle sat down in one. 'Very comfortable.
And what a view there is from your dining table.'

'About the one thing I really enjoy about this
flat is the view—it's why I moved in.'

Certainly he'd done nothing to impede it. There
were no curtains, only plain Holland blinds. The
room was L-shaped, and in this arm where they
were there was only the big pine table and chairs.
In the other arm there was a big couch covered in
oatmeal tweed and a scattering of what Robert
informed her were safari chairs. 'A silly descrip-
tion, but I rather took to them.' He grinned. 'I saw
them in the barn one day, too.' The chairs had pine
frames and oatmeal-tweed cushions, and Gabrielle
took to them, too. Along almost every wall that
wasn't window there were tall white bookshelves,
and apart from that there was a battered and
amazingly friendly old desk, covered in papers and
files and copies of the *BMJ* and *Lancet*.

'I love it,' she told him.

'Nice of you to say so.'

He'd gone formal and distant again, she thought
regretfully. Had she been too enthusiastic?

'Let me get you a drink,' he was saying. 'What
are you on?'

'Just dry vermouth, thank you.'

'Ice and lemon?'

'Please.'

He disappeared into what she realised must be

the kitchen. Doors opened and shut, and he reappeared with her drink, ice-cold and clinking.

She took the heavy crystal tumbler in her hands, and looked round the room again. 'Tell me about this barn,' she said. 'If all this furniture would be at home in it, it must be quite something.'

He sat down opposite her at the pine table, his own drink held in long narrow fingers. His eyes lit up, and she saw she'd hit on some loved project of his, so far unsuspected by the unit.

'It is,' he said. 'I bought it for a song, years back. It's near Bramley House—that's how I discovered it. It was no more than a shell, but luckily with planning permission, and I've been gradually restoring it. Except that you can hardly call it restoration. There was nothing to restore. Just a huge barn, with an old tiled roof coming nearly down to ground level on one side, and an enormous empty interior with thick oak beams. I've worked on it at weekends and holidays for five years now, with the aid of a local joiner, who's the brains behind it all. I'm no more than his unskilled mate.' What he didn't explain was how at one time he'd imagined Lucilla helping him to turn the barn into a home where he'd imagined their children running wild all summer through. 'Luckily for me,' he went on, 'the roof timbers were sound. The first two years we spent putting in a damp course and a quarry-tiled floor. I thought that would never be finished.' He smiled reminiscently. 'Recently I've installed a few amenities—at one stage I used to stay there each weekend using a sleeping bag on a mound of hay, and washing at a tap in the yard. I've running water inside now, and an immersion heater. Luxury.' He grinned again, and looked, she thought, years younger, and not frightening at all. 'Electric light, I have, too. and night storage heaters as well as a slow combustion stove. I bought some army surplus beds, and the place'll sleep six now. Apart from that, though, there's an old door propped on trestles for a table, and a few deck chairs to sit on.'

Gabrielle found it curiously peaceful and relaxing to sit at Robert's pine table staring out at the view of London beyond his dark head, while he talked on about this barn of his in the depths of the country. She was, however briefly, safely established in a world where there was no Paul, no Anik, and where even her Membership failure could temporarily be ignored. She allowed her eyes to dwell on Robert's lean figure as he sat turning his tumbler in his hands, his eyes alight, his face vivid with fast-changing expressions. She would never have thought of describing her chief as a restful personality. Rather the contrary. Yet to be with him like this was amazingly healing.

He might be telling her about his barn, but he remained one of the most astute clinicians in the Central. He watched her, saw the tension beginning to leave her, the pain in her eyes lessening. Go on, he said to himself, go on about the barn. Keep off medicine. Keep off all her problems.

'Luckily,' he ploughed on, 'all the timbers were sound. Strong old English oak. Otherwise I'd have been on a hiding to nothing. The roof timbers are fantastic, you know. There's genuine beauty there. So I want to retain the open roof always. To make this practicable, I've partitioned off a couple of rooms on the ground floor at either end. Two bedrooms at one end, and at the other a kitchen and bathroom and another small room. Eventually I plan to have stairs and make galleries above these rooms, but I haven't got round to that yet. In winter, though, it's at last possible to live comfortably in the partitioned-off rooms without attempting to heat the soaring roof space—which is where all the heat used to go.'

'It sounds wonderful. I'd love to see it.' She halted abruptly. Had she gone too far, cadging an invitation?

Apparently not. 'Easy enough,' he said. 'I'll take you one Saturday if you like, after a clinic. Only a step from Bramley House. You can come along and we'll have a picnic there instead of lunch in the dining room. It's pretty spartan, though, I warn you.' The prospect elated him, though he couldn't imagine why. Mention of a picnic, however, gave him another idea. 'Would you like to stay here and eat by any chance? Rather than bother to go out again? It would be easy enough—I've a full freezer.'

'I must say, if you wouldn't mind, I'd be thankful to stay put. I feel as if I could stay here for ever, looking at your view, and doing nothing.'

'Right. You do that, and I'll put something in the oven.'

'Can I do anything?'

'Not a thing.'

Robert returned to the kitchen, where once again doors opened and shut. He didn't consult her about the meal, but when it came it was delicious. They ate at his big table, with the strains of Bach from his record player filling the room and the lights of London standing out against a blue-black sky. They drank Hock, dry and flowery in the mouth, cool and refreshing, out of heavy crystal glasses, a narrower version of the tumbler in which he'd given her the vermouth.

'I admire your glasses,' she told him. 'Did you order them by telephone too?

'No. They were a leaving present from my last hospital. Danish.'

'You know, I envy you in a way, being able to choose from any number of modern designs like this. I have a certain amount of furniture from my grandmother's house that I do treasure—I'd never want to get rid of it. She had some lovely glass, too, which I'm lucky to possess. Anything extra I buy, though, does rather have to fit in with what I've got.' She ate the last mouthful of the iced consommé that he had assured her came out of a tin, though she found this difficult to believe. 'I think you're quite wrong about this flat being in the least like a hostel.'

'Impersonal, then. Needs something to bring it to life, give it humanity.' He stared intently at her, thinking that all it turned out to need was Gabrielle. Sitting here at his table, drinking his wine, and eating his food, she illuminated his bleak flat with her own beauty. While she was with him his distaste for the place vanished. He rose to his feet, and collecting her bowl and his own returned to the kitchen, from which a most savoury aroma had been emanating for some while. 'Only fish pie,' he informed her to her surprise, when he returned with two steaming plates. 'But rather a special one knocked up by Marks & Spencer, to which I'm distinctly partial. Marvellous late night snack.' He placed her plate before her, and went back for a big wooden bowl of salad. 'Help yourself.'

Gabrielle had supposed she was off food, might never eat again after her horrible news of failure, but suddenly she was ravenous. She covered her plate with crisp lettuce, while Robert poured more of the cool refreshing Hock into her glass. She took up her fork, and attacked the fish pie. 'Fantastic. What a find. I must get this into my freezer, too. I can imagine, when you come back late and tired, it must be just the thing.'

He watched her eating, and wondered why on earth she fascinated him so. She was no more, he reminded himself, than an unhappy girl who'd just failed the Membership through her own bad management, and whom he'd brought back out of duty. She sat here at his pine table, and he couldn't take his eyes off her. There she was, forking up mouthfuls of fish pie. She had beautiful hands. Long-fingered and sensitive. He wanted to take them into his own and hold them for ever.

This would never do.

'More salad?'

'Salad? Yes, thank you, I will.'

As though hypnotised, his eyes slid back, watched her fingers handling his wooden salad servers, picking up the crisp green lettuce, depositing it on her plate.

'A few plants would do a lot for this room, if you insist it needs livening up,' she commented.

'What sort of plants?' Not that he cared. He'd lost interest in the flat. It was, after all, no more than a roof over his head, a machine for living in.

For making love in.

'Big plants.'

She was answering him. He'd better listen, instead of allowing his body to take over and make all these suggestions that there could be no question, no question whatsoever, of its being allowed to carry out. 'Er—big plants?'

'Yes. Things like that Gruyère cheese plant—what do they call it? Monstera? Or is that something else?' Her huge grey eyes regarded him interrogatively.

He longed to give her an answer that would surprise her. 'Monstera?' he heard himself repeat, like some idiot student on a ward round.

'I think it may be. Yes—Monstera deliciosa, that's it. And then you could have that vine, the kangaroo vine, cissus antarctica. That's very easy, and it spreads like mad. It would soon festoon the windows.' Her eyes took on a far-away look. 'Two big plants standing there, either side of the middle window, in big white pots. I can see them.'

'M—hm.'

She came back to herself with a jolt. 'You'd have to keep on watering them, of course. Would you remember to do that?'

'I see no reason why not.' He was curt. 'Ready for coffee?' Without waiting for her answer, he went through to the kitchen.

Now he'd taken offence. When he'd been so kind up to then. In her turn, she stood up, collected the two plates and the salad bowl, and followed him for the first time into the kitchen. The least she could do was to take the plates out. She'd been eating and drinking, waited on by him, all evening.

He was not pleased to see her. The last thing he wanted was her warm soft sexy body brushing up against him in the narrow galley kitchen.

'No need for that.' There was a cutting edge to his tone of which he was unaware. 'I can manage a spot of coffee unassisted, thanks very much.' Go away, go away, he meant. Go away before I grab you and everything spins out of control. 'Go and sit down—try the sofa. Relax.' Relax? Who was supposed to relax, for God's sake? He was the one who needed relaxation.

Hurt and unnerved, Gabrielle went quietly away, past the pine table in the window where she'd been, briefly, so surprisingly and entirely happy, over to the big oatmeal-tweed sofa, on the edge of which she perched insecurely, wishing she hadn't somehow offended and annoyed him.

However, when he reappeared with two steaming mugs of delicious coffee, she was relieved to find that he appeared to have regained his temper.

He sat down, not on the sofa next to her, which would have been friendly, she thought, but perhaps too much to ask, but opposite, in one of the low-slung chairs. 'Yes,' he said amiably. 'I see what you mean. A bit of greenery in tubs by the windows would do a lot for this room.'

Thankful to have him in an approachable mood again, she agreed fervently.

'Where would I get them?'

'Oh, the florist in Great St Anne's would have them, I'm sure.'

'Would you come with me and help me choose them?'

'Of course. I'd love to.'

He smiled suddenly, the wide transfiguring smile that so altered his face, making him seem all at once young and friendly and the easiest person to be with, instead of the most difficult.

'That's a date, then.'

'Sure.' Happy again, she smiled back at him.

Robert reminded himself fiercely about his father-figure role. She sat there on his sofa, this lovely, desirable girl—no, that would never do. This poor girl on his staff who had just failed the Membership. And fortunately his recipe had worked. She seemed relaxed, no longer tearing herself apart over either the Membership or Paul

Singh. He was the one who was doing the agonising now. But if he had succeeded in giving her an evening's respite from her problems, that was enough. What he must do next was to see that she remained in this comparatively easy-going frame of mind and then went home and had a good night's sleep. The coffee he'd made was decaffeinated, though he hadn't told her so. What he had to do was find some non-challenging subject to keep her occupied until he took her home for an early night and a good rest.

'You're good at making a home,' he said. 'Your own flat is charming. I remember when I came to that party of yours how welcoming it seemed.' Hell, he shouldn't have reminded her of the engagement party. He'd boobed. Get away from the subject fast. 'So what else would you do to make this flat more of a home?' He didn't really care, but she'd never suspect that. This flat was all right, really. The furniture he'd bought was functional and quite adequate, all the place had needed was another human being besides himself. That stopped it being cold and empty. A lovely girl with huge grey eyes and a wonderful body. Again he wrenched his thoughts into different channels. 'My sister came here once and said what it needed was splashes of colour.'

'Oh, I love the pale look. But if you—it depends what colours you like. What *are* your colours!' Sitting in Robert Scorer's flat, asking him about his favourite colours. Who would have believed it?

Apparently he had no idea. 'I don't care for all

those dingy shades people go in for. Those muddy colours.'

Gabrielle rose to her feet and wandered about, looking at the room from different angles. 'You could have green, to go with the plants, one green wall.'

Plainly he was not transported.

'Or yellow,' she suggested. 'Pale lemon yellow would keep it cool and fresh, yet liven it up no end. Lemon walls, lemon cushions and a lemon rug. Rather pleasant?'

His expression was unreadable.

Assuming his inscrutability indicated lack of approval, which it did not—he was immensely approving of her own shape as she moved about his room, and was engaged in fighting yet another battle with himself—Gabrielle resumed her search for a colour to please him. 'Orange?' she asked herself. 'A vivid orange?' She turned the idea down out of hand. 'No, it wouldn't do. You'd lose this lovely cool spacious feeling the room has. You know, I don't think it does really need colour. How about black-and-white cushions for a bit of drama, and leave it at that?'

He blinked. 'Black-and-white cushions?' His expression remained indecipherable.

Belatedly, Gabrielle grasped what was wrong. She was boring him blind. She glanced at her watch. 'Me for an early night,' she exclaimed. 'I must go. Thank you for being so patient—and for not once telling me what you think of me for making a mess of the Membership.'

He was on his feet. 'Don't think about it. Nothing to be done tonight or tomorrow. So just don't dwell on it, will you? Pointless expenditure of energy. Turn your back on your problems, have a good night's sleep, and in a day or two you'll see —everything will be quite manageable.'

Privately she doubted this. But it would be ungrateful to say so, and in any case he was absolutely right about tonight. Tonight she was going to follow his advice and conduct no post-mortem. 'I've had a really super evening—all that marvellous food, too—and I feel quite different.'

'Good,' he said mildly. 'That was the idea. Now I'll walk you home.'

'Oh, please don't bother. I—'

'Of course I will.' He ushered her out of his flat over her protests, into his streamlined lift that flashed lights at them and sucked them down to the main lobby, which, Gabrielle noticed, had great pots of Monstera deliciosa standing about.

'That's it. That's the plant I mean.'

'Oh, that. Well, I suppose I could.' He sounded more than dubious, and Gabrielle spent the short walk round the corner trying to convince him she was right. As soon as they reached her flat he stopped in his tracks, wished her a curt good night, sketched one of his lightning salutes, and turned on his heel.

CHAPTER SIX

As Gabrielle was climbing into bed, sleepily wondering if deep purple cushions and one purple wall would be a success in Robert's flat, the telephone rang.

She picked it up reluctantly, praying they didn't want her on the ward.

Paul. And not before time, she thought, though at this hour he might really have left it until the morning.

'Where *have* you been?' he demanded.

'Robert Scorer took me out to a meal.' She was irritated. Where had she been indeed. Didn't he care that she had bloody well failed the Membership and, what's more, if it had not been for Robert, would have been alone all evening facing that fact?

Paul had forgotten about the Membership. 'I've been trying to get you for hours,' he said. 'Anik is on her way.'

'*What*?'

'She's on her way. My uncle had a cable from my father. She's arriving at Heathrow tomorrow morning—I have to meet her.'

Gabrielle stared unseeingly at the telephone in her hand.

'Gaby? I said Anik—'

91

'Yes, I heard. What are you going to do?'

'Meet her. I have to.'

'I didn't mean that. I meant—well, about us.'

'Us? This is nothing to do with you and me. I thought we were agreed on that. I shall simply meet her and take her to Ledford. That's all.'

'But of course it affects us. We must face it, Paul. If she's here and staying with your aunt and uncle, we can't pretend it makes no difference.'

'I don't see why it should. We were agreed that it was right to let her come to the UK and take her course. She's come earlier than we expected, unfortunately. But it doesn't affect you and me. Not in any way.'

'But it does. It must do. After all, you can't have two fiancées underfoot.' Gabrielle, to her fury, gave what she intended to be an airy little laugh, only to find it emerge as a loud and unmistakable sob. She put her hand over the mouthpiece before Paul could hear it, swallowed twice, and said in a rigidly controlled voice, 'Anyway, we won't discuss it now. Far too late. If you have to meet her tomorrow morning, you must do that, and take her to Ledford. Afterwards we can talk.' Gabrielle might feel as if she were in an unending nightmare, but her voice gave not the slightest indication of this. She had it under complete control again, and sounded very much as she might have done on the ward or in sister's office, deciding what should be done next and who should do it.

Paul suspected nothing. 'I'll ring you when I get back, then,' he said, relieved.

'Yes, do that.' She put the telephone down. This was unbelievable. The entire day had been unbelievable. The collapse of her hopes for the Membership, the evening in Robert's flat, and now this.

Paul's aunt had spelt out to her what would be involved if Anik came to stay with them. They would sponsor her as Paul's future wife.

What she herself had said on the telephone just now was no more than the truth. The exact truth. He could not have two fiancées underfoot. She had to act. At once. Barefoot, in her lacy nightdress she walked through to the sitting room, sat down at her desk and wrote to Paul ending their engagement.

The letter, to her horror when she reread it, was a cry of anguish and a pathetic plea for support and understanding, enumerating not only her own misery about Anik, but her despair at having failed the Membership.

Disgusted, she tore it in small pieces and began again. Her second effort came out as a formal and stilted little note, saying no more than that she regarded their engagement as at an end. She read it through, scowled at it. Brief and to the point. That was all you could say for it. It would have to do. She was not going to sit at her desk all night making up suitable letters to end her engagement. She put it in an envelope, sealed it, addressed it. She'd leave it in the office for him to find when he came back to the hospital.

She put her head down on her desk and wept.

* * *

The following morning she felt a wreck. She shrugged. Nothing to be done. She climbed into a newly-pressed skirt, put on her most tailored shirt, brushed her hair and screwed it into the tightest and most long-lasting of knots, made her face up with obsessional care. That was that. She was tidy and neat, and if make-up failed adequately to disguise her sunken eyes and drawn features, and the blusher she'd used with such expertise, she'd imagined, stood out against her pasty complexion like a clown's make-up, it couldn't be helped. That was the best she could do. She wasn't in modelling, anyway. If they didn't like the way she looked they could get lost. Too bad.

As she made her way to the office to leave Paul's note, she caught a lot of sidelong glances, but she ignored them, collected her own case notes and papers and began her day.

She was settling outstanding details with the sister after her round when Robert Scorer appeared at her elbow.

'If you could spare me a minute, Dr Vereker.' His tone was formal, his eye quelling.

'Of course, sir.' Now what?

They walked together to the landing, and paused.

'What the hell have you been doing since I left you last night?' he demanded. 'You look like death warmed up.'

Marvellous. Just what she needed to make her day. 'Thanks so much,' she snapped back sarcastically.

'So what has happened?' He enunciated every word separately, as though she were the most moronic house officer he'd encountered in his entire career.

Gabrielle opened her mouth to demolish him, even if he was her chief and she ruined what remained of her career.

'I suppose it's Paul Singh again,' he told her, before she had thought up a sufficiently devastating phrase to cut him down to size.

She gulped, and to her disgust felt a sob rising exactly as it had done the previous night on the telephone. She fought it back, nodded mutely.

'God in heaven.' He sounded as despairing as she felt, and her anger evaporated, leaving only, to her embarrassment, an increasing compulsion to burst into tears. 'What is it *now*?'

She muttered hurriedly that Anik had arrived. Paul was meeting her at Heathrow and taking her to Ledford.

Robert exploded. 'That's all it needs.'

Gabrielle, damp-eyed, nodded. That about summed it up.

'Look here.' He was angry again. 'You've got to get away. What you need is a break. Somewhere quiet.'

She nodded again. That was it. That was what she needed. To be anywhere but here. To be somewhere else. Where Paul and Anik couldn't descend on her. Where she couldn't be expected to do anything about them. Or anything else, for that matter.

'Tell you what,' he said. 'You'd better come down to Bramley House with me. Got my Saturday morning clinic, and I'm driving down tonight, taking a couple of students. We're staying overnight at that barn I told you about.'

Gabrielle nodded. She seemed to have given up speaking, she thought hopelessly. All she could do was nod like some mechanical toy.

'The students are doing the clinic with me, and then a round in the afternoon. You can have a lie-in and a quiet day on your own at the barn. Lying in the sun, if there is any. All right?'

She nodded again.

'Meet you in the King's Head about six-thirty. You're not going to do any clinic or round, so wear jeans and walking shoes, or something like that. Bring an anorak. Nothing else.'

She nodded.

'Right. Six-thirty.' He departed downstairs at a run.

Punctually at six-thirty, carrying her zipped weekend case, Gabrielle entered the King's Head. Robert waved to her from the bar, and she pushed her way through to join him there.

'We're having a snack here before we leave,' he told her. 'Easier. I'm having roast beef and salad —that do for you?'

'Thank you, that'd be fine.' At present, Gabrielle didn't really care if she never ate again. Her appetite had deserted her. She knew better, though, than to inform her chief of this.

'Another roast beef,' he said. 'No, hold it. Better

make it four while you're at it. We'll take a chance on the other two being satisfied with that. What'll you drink?'

'Drink?' A pint of brandy, for a total knock-out, was all that came to Gabrielle's mind. 'Perhaps a shandy,' she said weakly.

'Look as if you need something a good deal stronger.' He scrutinised her unflatteringly. 'Ever drink Guinness?'

'I have done, yes.' Gran used to drink it, and Gabrielle had sometimes shared a bottle with her and found to her surprise that she enjoyed the flavour.

'A Black Velvet,' he told the barman. 'Two halves of bitter, and four coffees. There's a table free now,' he added. 'Over there. Go and occupy it, there's a good girl.'

When he joined her he had the two students with him, and between them they were carrying all the drinks and the beef, as well as rolls and butter all round. Gabrielle already knew Martin Elsworthy and Alison Gilbert, both fifth-year students, and when they had sorted out their food and drink, the talk soon settled into the usual unit chat about patients and drug dosages, though Gabrielle did interrupt it to enquire what was in her Guinness. 'It's very nice, but it isn't just Guinness, is it?'

'Black Velvet, I ordered. You heard me. That's champagne and Guinness.'

'I shall probably keel over as soon as I get outside,' she protested. 'Not even make your car.'

'Three of us here,' Robert said cheerfully. 'We

can support you. And you can sleep in the car. All three of you can, in fact.'

'It seems a bit unfair, if we all snore our heads off, while you drive,' Alison said.

'I shall survive on my own thoughts.'

Robert was his usual acerbic self, Gabrielle reflected. Amazing how he could be the soul of kindness one minute, and then bite their heads off.

Somewhat to her surprise, she did fall asleep, and only woke as the car bumped gently to a halt on a cart track by the barn. 'You don't mean we're here?' She peered at Robert from sleepy grey eyes and tumbled hair, looking more like one of the children at Bramley House than a senior house officer from the Central London Hospital. He was tempted to pick her up like one of the children, carry her into the barn and tuck her up in bed.

However, he had to unlock the place and switch on the water and electricity before he could hope to embark on this programme, and by then she was on her feet, breathing in great gulps of country air. 'It smells marvellous,' she said. 'Altogether different. London air is so stale and dead.'

He picked up her zip bag. 'Come on. You're for bed, stat.' He led the way into the old building, and turned off into a room on his right.

Gabrielle had a vague impression of rafters towering above her before she followed him into what was, in fact, the room he usually slept in himself, with more in the way of amenities than any other. He dumped her bag by the small single bed, switched on a two-bar electric fire and an anglepoise lamp on a shelf beside the bed, gestured at a wall cupboard, said 'you can hang your stuff in there. I'll get you a sleeping bag.'

'Oh, but can't I—?' She was addressing empty space.

He was back quickly, with a sleeping bag, a pillow and a sheet sleeping bag of a type familiar to Gabrielle from youth hostelling days. 'There you are. I think that's everything. Now listen to me.'

As if she had the opportunity to do anything else.

'Go straight to bed, and stay there. Alison'll bring you some hot milk, when we've unpacked a bit. Tomorrow—'

'But you must let me help with the unpacking.'

'Three of us can handle it. Go to bed. And in the morning stay there. One of us will bring you some tea before we go, and we shan't be back until some time in the afternoon. Sleep late, don't attempt to do anything like cleaning or cooking, or I'll scalp you. I want to find this place exactly as I leave it, and I shall spot it if you've done so much as rinse out a cup. It's a simple place, and I know every inch of it, don't forget. I've brought you down here for a rest, and that's what you're going to have. All right?'

'Thank you very much. Surely I—'

'Stay in bed as long as you can, then get yourself some lunch. Apart from that, go for a walk, or sit in the sun, if there should be any. Nothing else.

Bathroom's next door, kitchen next to that. See you tomorrow. Night.' He was gone.

Gabrielle unpacked, washed, and climbed into the sleeping bags. She hardly had time to wonder what it was he'd said about hot milk when Alison knocked and appeared with a steaming pottery mug.

'Here you are,' she said cheerfully. 'Sir says to remind you you're not to move in the morning. I'll bring you some tea. You OK?'

'Fine, thanks. A bit guilty about not having helped with any unpacking.'

'Not to worry. Martin and I are used to this trip now, we have it taped. See you around eight-thirty.' She too was gone.

The mug proved to contain Horlick's, made to the creamy consistency favoured on the wards, sweet and malty, immensely comforting. Stupefying, too. Gabrielle could hardly keep a hold on consciousness long enough to swallow the final mouthfuls.

She returned to hazy awareness to find Alison back with a mug of tea and a plate of buttered toast.

'Just off,' she said brightly, dumped the tea and toast on the shelf by the bed, and departed.

Gabrielle sipped the tea, and munched buttery toast. Delicious. She yawned, and dropped off to sleep again.

She could hardly believe her watch when she next woke. Midday. She wriggled out of the sleeping bags, clicked up the blind. Sunlight lay on swathes of grass on a hillside.

The window was a small lattice fitted between the oak beams of the barn's structure, a charming narrow hole in the wall. Gabrielle wondered what it felt like to be Robert Scorer and turn a barn into a home.

A home, she reminded herself, with hot and cold running water. She padded through to the bathroom, lay soaking in hot water, relaxed and dreamy, and then rubbed herself dry on a bright blue towel, pulled on jeans and her checked shirt, brushed out her hair and left it loose on her shoulders, slipped into her sandals and went exploring.

The beauty of the barn took her breath away. Age-old rafters climbed dizzily above her, their lines broken only by the tall chimney stack of the slow-combustion stove. Light poured in from what must once have been the great entrance doors for wagons, now offering a wide view of the downs and the sea in the distance.

She let herself out through a door alongside the huge expanse of window, and found herself on a flagstoned rectangle with, awaiting her invitingly, deck chairs. The day was sunny, though there was a brisk wind blowing from the sea. She went in, put on a sweater, came out again, and lay back in a deck chair. The wind ruffled her hair and the sun warmed her. She began to feel mindlessly sensuous, her thoughts absent, her eyes exploring the hills and the blue line of sea.

Hunger, though, at last drove her back into the kitchen. This, though functional, was clearly

unfinished. Stranded round the walls and connec-
ted by a framework of joists were a stainless steel
sink, an electric cooker and a refrigerator. Sitting
on top of the refrigerator was a note. 'G. Ham and
salad in fridge, or bacon and egg if preferred.
Bread, apples and oranges around. RS.'

Brief and to the point, like most of his communi-
cations.

Suddenly ravenous, she cut herself slices of ham,
added potato salad from a carton, helped herself
to lettuce and tomatoes, and poured a mug of
creamy milk.

Out again to the flagstones in the sun and the
wind, where she polished off her plateful surprisingly quickly, and went back to the kitchen to
make coffee. Once there, though, she hesitated.
What about washing up? Apart from her own
plates and mugs, there was a pile of crockery in
the sink. She put on the kettle for coffee, and
pondered. Was she so cowed she'd leave the washing up because she was afraid of what Robert
would say when he came back?

She made her coffee, took an apple, and
returned to her deck chair. She wasn't sure whether
she was cowed or simply lazy, but it seemed a pity
to miss the sun by washing up in the kitchen only
to be bawled out by Robert.

When the car eventually turned in at the gate
into the field, he was alone. He parked at the side
of the barn, and came across to join her.

'You look a good deal better,' he told her.

'I feel it. I've had a wonderful day doing nothing.

I haven't even washed up.' This continued to bother her.

'Told you I'd scalp you if you lifted a finger. Meant it.' His eyes scrutinised her. In jeans and sweater, a battered pair of old sandals, her hair loose on her shoulders, she looked nothing but a teenager, he thought. A vulnerable teenager, whom he was going to look after, as much as if she had been a patient at Bramley House. He subdued the promptings of his body, a creature of only one idea where attractive girls were involved. For Gabrielle, nothing more than affectionate concern was to be permitted.

'How about a cup of tea?' he asked.

'Be great. Let me—'

'You stay where you are. I'll get it. I'll bring in some more stuff from the car first, though—by the way, I promised to collect Alison and Martin from Southbridge between nine and ten. They're going to have a meal in the Rose & Crown there. Don't let me forget, will you? I thought we could eat here—I bought a lettuce and some potatoes. We can finish off the ham, with salad and potatoes baked in their jackets.'

'Sounds delicious,' she said, but only to his rear view. He was already moving back to the car. He collected a carton of provisions and went into the barn, to emerge shortly in jeans and a fisherman's sweater, carrying two mugs of tea in one hand and a tin of biscuits in the other. They sat companionably sipping tea and talking idly about Martin and Alison, about Bramley House and one or two cases there Robert was planning to bring back into the Central for intensive treatment. Then, his mug empty, he rose. 'Care for a short walk on the downs?'

'Love one.'

'After that I want to do a spot of carpentry before supper.'

'So you'll at least allow me to put the potatoes in the oven and wash the lettuce,' she urged.

He grinned. He looked years younger, and suddenly, unheralded, her awe of him vanished, to be replaced by an uprush of genuine affection.

'I might, at that,' he agreed, looking down at her, repressing his urge to take her into his arms and make love to her. 'After our walk, that is. Come on.'

On the chalky uplands, the wind blew their hair and the distances stretched their eyes, as they swung along, talking partly about the patients he'd seen that morning and partly about local landmarks. To walk together in the wind from the sea, talking away easily about anything or nothing seemed the most natural thing in the world, and both of them were happy.

They came back to the barn, and Gabrielle made for the kitchen. 'I'm going to see about supper.' She issued the statement as a challenge.

Robert chuckled. 'OK, you win. I'll start on my carpentry.'

From the kitchen, as she scrubbed potatoes, washed lettuce and then determinedly began on the forbidden washing up, she could hear him sawing away, and an hour later, when the potatoes were cooked and supper ready, she had the greatest difficulty in detaching him from his carpentry. Only the sight and smell of his potato, halved and buttered, waved under his nose on its plate, finally drew him to eat.

Since the only table was now covered in wood and shavings, they ate with their plates on their knees in the great window looking out on to the downs and the distant sea, while Robert, in the grip of his enthusiasm, explained to her in detail what he was making—a worktop, shelves and then eventually cupboard doors for the kitchen. Finally she had to remind him of the time.

'Nearly nine-thirty, I'm afraid. And you said—'

'Lord, yes. I must go and collect those two from Southbridge. Like to come? We can have a drink with them in the Rose & Crown before we come back.'

'I'd love that.'

They drove along winding country lanes in the light of an apricot sunset into a small town with a wide main street of Georgian terraces. In the Rose & Crown the bar was packed with Saturday-night drinkers, but Martin and Alison waved from a small table under a window, and they took their drinks over to join them. The talk at once became indistinguishable from that of any coffee break after Outpatients or a ward round at the Central. They didn't stay long, though. Robert decreed early bed for everyone.

'I want to make an early start in the morning,'

he told them. 'I'd like to be able to finish my
worktops this weekend.'

Gabrielle was a little relieved to find that he
didn't propose to start again the moment they
reached the barn—she wouldn't have put it past
him to finish his worktops by sawing through the
night.

Once they were back, he turned on her. 'Gaby,
you're first for the bathroom. You're the one supposed to be catching up on your sleep.'

'Hurry up, and I'll bring you some Horlick's.'
Alison immediately backed him up.

Lying in her sleeping bags, letting what remained
of her tension slide from her, Gabrielle hugged to
herself the memory of Robert calling her Gaby
for the first time. It seemed encouraging. Not to
mention promising. What she meant by that she
didn't stop to examine. But her last picture before
she drifted off to sleep was of Robert in his white
fisherman's sweater, striding along the uplands
with her in the sunlight.

CHAPTER SEVEN

ON SUNDAY morning Gabrielle woke to the crashing back of her door, accompanied by Robert's entry, speaking as he came. 'Mug of tea for you. Eight o'clock. Want to make an early start.' The mug clicked down—almost inside her ear, it seemed—on the bedside shelf while, half a second later, her blind clicked up and light flooded the room. 'Not a very promising morning,' he told her. 'Grey. Drizzly. Pity.' The door shut and he had gone.

Gabrielle sat up. Make an early start, he'd said, last night and again this morning. So on no account must she allow herself to drop off to sleep. She pushed the sleeping bags down, extricated herself, and sat on the side of the bed sipping her tea. Delicious. Hot, though. Not to be downed at one gulp.

Feeling rather as though she were a very raw recruit at a tough training depot who'd been roused by a terrifying sergeant major, she began to dress fast. She had no glimpse of the battle Robert had had with himself in order not to linger by her bed harbouring any number of delightful and unsuitable notions, like somehow finding room in her sleeping bag for both of them.

Pulling on jeans and sweater, pausing momentarily to sip her tea, by the time Gabrielle was fully

dressed she was also wide awake. She slipped
through to the bathroom to complete the good work
by splashing her face in cold water, and then went
into the huge raftered living-room, where she found
Robert standing frowning over his table, engrossed
in some calculation between his ruler and the back
of an envelope. He glanced up as she approached,
and looked surprised. 'You've been fast.'

So could she have stayed in bed for hours, and
he wouldn't have minded? Hell.

'I thought I'd get breakfast.'

'Splendid.' He was hearty, and she never
guessed how much he was longing to drop his ruler,
come round the table and take her into his arms.

'Bacon and egg?' She was tentative, expecting
him to bite her head off and inform her crisply that
there was no time to waste.

Instead he smiled the sudden lopsided crinkly
smile that so changed his face. 'Terrific. If you can
be bothered.'

'Of course I can be bothered,' she snapped. 'I've
hardly lifted a finger since I arrived. I can rustle
up a bit of breakfast without killing myself, I should
hope.' The kitchen door slammed behind her.

So what was that in aid of, you moron, she asked
herself on the other side of it? What on earth had
got into her?

Robert knew exactly what had got into her. She
might look rested, but she was still overwrought.
He longed to be able to put everything right for
her, but there was nothing he could do. Her trouble
was Paul, and nothing he, Robert Scorer, who was

beginning to fear he loved her desperately, could do or say would ease her pain in the slightest. All he could offer was a brief respite, accompanied by the typical physician's prescription of rest, fresh air and good food. He sighed, wanting to take her into his arms and tell her he was going to look after her and everything would be all right. He snorted. He could imagine what Gabrielle would have to say about that. What was more, she'd be right. All he could do to help her was to clear his carpentry off the table so that it was ready for her breakfast, and hustle up Martin and Alison to eat it.

At the meal, they announced they were hoping to go for a long walk over the downs. Was it going to drizzle all day, or might it clear up? Throughout breakfast they made trips first to stare out of the big window on the west side and then to the small window on the north side, to gauge what the north wind was bringing with it, apart from the un-seasonal chill. Finally they decided to take a chance on the weather, and Robert offered to give them a lift as far as the downs footpath a couple of miles past Bramley House.

'That would be super,' Alison said. 'But I thought you were going to stay here and finish your worktops?'

He nodded. 'That's right. But I'll have to check in at Bramley House this morning in case there are any messages. I'll have to do something soon about having a telephone installed here. It's nice and peaceful the way it is, but there's a price to be paid in these regular trips to and from Bramley House.'

By nine-thirty the three of them had departed, and Gabrielle was washing up. After this she decided to risk Robert's disapproval by making a warming soup for lunch. They could have it with cheese at any stage from midday to three in the afternoon, which surely would not menace his carpentry too much.

. What menaced his carpentry turned out to be his absence. Eleven o'clock came, and then twelve, and he had not returned.

At twelve-thirty he reappeared, curt and irritable. 'So much for my early start. They'd a problem in the wards in London, and I had to wait while they got hold of Haddow, so that he could give me a report. Thought I might have to go up this afternoon, but luckily it seems not to be necessary after all.'

'Would you like lunch early, so that you can get in a long afternoon on the worktops? I've made some soup, and there's cheese.'

'Good plan. Then we can clear the table and I can cut out that final corner piece. After that I'll be able to start assembling it.'

Gabrielle expected him to tell her during lunch what the problem in the ward was—after all, she worked there too, even if she was a mere senior house officer and he the director of the unit. She had a right to be told. But he said nothing, talked on about his plans for the barn.

He'd switched off, she decided, from that morning's trouble. Completely. It was a gift most doctors acquired, and that she was badly in need of herself. If she'd done a bit more switching off, she'd have passed the Membership.

What she didn't know was that Robert was deliberately holding back from telling her about his morning. At Bramley House they had informed him that Dr Singh had been trying to reach him.

Robert had spoken to Paul, who was worried about a patient running a high temperature on top of a heart condition. Could he start her on an antibiotic? And if so, which one?

Robert thought Paul should have been capable of deciding this for himself. Failing that, he could have asked the unit's senior registrar. With some acerbity, he'd pointed this out, and Paul had promised to do so. By then, though, Robert felt he had to wait by the telephone until he had a report himself from the senior registrar, who had to travel in from his home in South London, examine the patient, hear the history from Paul and the house physician, talk to the ward sister, prescribe the antibiotic—and only then telephone Robert.

Nothing out of the ordinary. Typical, in fact. But Robert was determined not to bring Paul's name up to Gabrielle, particularly not in order to condemn him for what he considered to be lack of initiative. In any case, he reminded himself, this over-caution of Paul's, this habit of seeking a second opinion at the first hint of any doubt, was going to make him a safe and reliable family doctor out in the sticks—as everyone at the Central united in imagining any place more than ten miles from Trafalgar Square to be.

He and Gabrielle sat in the big window, drinking coffee. Although earlier he'd been in such a hurry to begin on the worktops, he found that now all he wanted was to sit like this for ever, quietly spending time with this lovely girl of his. Not only was she beautiful, desirable and, God help him, irresistibly sexy. She was companionable. He wanted to live alongside her for the rest of his days.

She sat there, slim legs crossed, wearing jeans, a cream shirt—yesterday, he remembered, it had been some sort of check—and on this grey and chilly day a pale blue sweater. He was experiencing a growing devotion to her. If he didn't watch it, it would take him over and run him. He ached at this moment to get his hands on her and make love to her.

Why not? They were alone in the barn for hours. Until dark, very likely. Uninterrupted.

He stood up. 'Time for my worktops.'

Gabrielle nodded. 'I'll clear away and wash up.'

On this occasion he made no attempt to stop her, and as she stacked plates in the kitchen she heard him begin sawing. She pushed her sleeves up and ran the water.

She was wiping round the top of the cooker when he came into the kitchen. 'I'm ready to start installing the tops at last. Would you give me a hand to bring them through and fit them?'

'Of course.' She dried her hands, followed him out, took one end of a worktop and carried it to the kitchen. Together they fitted it alongside the cooker, and returned for the next, to put it on the other side, between the cooker and the sink.

Back and forth, until they were both hot and there were worktops right round the room.

'What a difference. Terrific.'

'They look all right, don't they? What's more, every one of them fits.' He gave her his glinting sidelong smile. 'I wasn't one hundred per cent sure they would.'

'But you've been so careful with all your measurements. Anyway, I would expect you to be absolutely accurate, and get it right first time.' She gave him a smile that warmed him through to his bones.

'Gaby—' he began.

She looked enquiring.

'I—we—' He stopped. Began again. 'I'll have to screw it into place now. Means a lot of drilling. I wonder, if I drill, do you think you—would you follow round behind and put in the screws?'

'Of course.' She was inordinately delighted. He was going to allow her to help him actually fix his beloved worktops.

Through the afternoon they worked hard and steadily until the job was completed. Tired and triumphant, they regarded the kitchen and then one another.

'Made it,' Robert said. 'Hope you're not worn out. My God, I brought you down here for a rest.'

'I've had a super time.'

'So have I.' She was a wonderful girl, and in spite of all his theories about taking care of her he'd worked her into the ground. She must be worn out.

He'd make it up to her somehow. Not, however, in the precise way his body was urging. That was not on. He'd take her out instead. The way girls expected to be taken out. He'd drive her some-where for a fabulous once-in-a-lifetime meal. 'Come on, we're going out for a meal.'

'A meal? Now?'

'Why not?'

'But I could make supper here. In the new kitchen.'

'No. After this marathon, you deserve to be waited on. Too late, I'm afraid, to book a table at the Plough in Upmor. They're always booked two deep on Sunday evening—anyway, we haven't a telephone, and I'm damned if I'm calling in at Bramley House again today. They'd be bound to find something for me to do. So it'll have to be the Rose & Crown. They do quite a good meal, though.'

She looked harassed. 'I've nothing to wear.'

'Come as you are. You look fantastic.'

'I—I'll just wash, and do my face, then.' She escaped to the bathroom and stared at herself in the tiny square of mirror propped up above the basin. He had said she looked fantastic. Robert Scorer had opened his mouth and told her she looked fantastic. What's more, he'd meant it. Her eyes stared widely back at her. What was hap-pening?

Precisely nothing, she told herself firmly. They'd spent a hard-working afternoon on his kitchen, and now he was going to take her out for a meal.

As a reward, and because he was guilty about having worked her so hard, after all his talk about deck chairs and not lifting a finger.

Not lifting a finger. She scrutinised her hands. Her hands had been helping Robert all afternoon. This was what life would be like, with Robert. Working together, in the wards and here, in this heavenly old building.

What could she be thinking about? She was imagining herself staying here with Robert, hidden away from all her problems, working with him at carpentry, of all crazy things. Paul, Anik, the Membership—all forgotten.

Being with Robert here was like coming home —to a home that until now she had not known she had. As though the father she could hardly remember had taken her into his care, as though her lost grandmother was with her again, staunch and loving. And yet it was like neither of those. Altogether different. She had a new, caring protector. Robert. Sturdy. Reliable. A tower of strength for ever.

Hastily she reminded herself that she had nothing of the sort. Robert Scorer was neither her father nor her grandmother. Her lips twitched at the absurdity. Instead he was her chief, a consultant at the Central London Hospital, with responsibilities to patients and numerous other staff besides herself. She merely happened to be the one who'd just failed the Membership and got her love life into a hopeless tangle. He, competent and aware, had picked up the pieces and carted her off for a recuperative weekend that happened to fit in with his existing programme.

His prescription had worked. She was already a different person. So she must take herself off his hands. Beginning now. She must pull herself together, do her face, and go out with him for a meal.

A perfectly ordinary meal. Meaning nothing. Like an incantation she repeated this to herself as she sat at his side in the car. A perfectly ordinary meal. She was driving into Southbridge on the way to a meal at the Rose & Crown where, only the previous evening, they'd been to fetch Martin and Alison. Robert was always ferrying staff about the countryside, and giving them meals or drinks here and there.

They drove along the winding lanes as they had done last night. Only now Gabrielle was longing for the drive never to end. If they could just drive for ever like this. It was all she asked.

They parked outside the Rose & Crown, went inside and up to the bar. Just the same as yesterday. Except that everything had changed.

They stood at the bar, and for a fleeting moment she felt Robert's arm come round her shoulder as he stood beside her. Just for a moment. Then it was gone, and he was leaning on the counter, ordering their drinks.

He left her at the same small table in the window they'd occupied the evening before while he went to see about booking a table.

'In about half an hour,' he told her when he returned.

'Oh, good.' She smiled at him.

He kicked himself for the fool he'd been. What on earth had possessed him to bring her here for this blasted meal? Why hadn't he simply taken her to bed in the barn, while they had the place to themselves? A long evening of loving might have completed her rest cure in the best possible way. It would have set her up and distanced her from Paul. Made her understand that there were other men in the world. So why hadn't he seized her when he had the chance?

Because, a voice from deep within informed him, to his enormous surprise, he was going to marry her. She wasn't some passing affair. She was going to be his love for ever. He was going to detach her from Paul, right enough, but not temporarily, not momentarily, not for a short weekend's sex. No, he was going to make love to this girl, but not until she was ready and wanting him. No matter what it cost him.

They walked through to the dining room, and began on a delicious country paté with crisp hot toast, and glasses of mellow burgundy from the Rose & Crown cellars, a good deal more famous locally than the kitchens would ever be.

Gammon with cranberry sauce, mushrooms and chips (a Rose & Crown stand-by) arrived, and Robert opened his campaign. 'Now, about Paul and this Indian girl,' he said.

Gabrielle found she was ready, suddenly, to discuss it all. 'Anik,' she said.

'Ah yes. You know—I've told you so before—

whatever happens in the long term, you really do owe yourself a registrar's post at the Central.'

She raised her eyebrows. 'If I could get one, after failing the Membership like that.'

'You'll take the Membership again, and pass.'

'I might not even get it the second time.'

'You'll get it if Paul gives you half a chance to work for it.'

Gabrielle was astonished to find she agreed whole-heartedly. It was Paul's fault she had not been able to concentrate, his responsibility she had failed. She halted herself in her tracks. She must not try to shift the blame.

'No,' she said. 'The failure was mine. No one else's. I could have done more work, and I didn't.'

Loyal and true, Robert told himself. Carrying all the blame herself, when it had been Paul's fault for landing too many emotional problems on her, at the worst possible moment. 'I told that bloody Paul,' he snapped, 'not to worry you. But he still came badgering you, didn't he, with his anxieties about that Indian girl?'

Gabrielle stared. Robert had told Paul not to worry her? He'd actually realised her difficulties, and warned Paul to—to lay off? Robert Scorer, so tight-lipped and unemotional, had not only seen what was happening to her, but had tried to do something about it. He'd tried to protect her.

She drank a mouthful of burgundy, ate a mushroom. Hell, she reminded herself fiercely, she must not look for protection from anyone. She must

look after herself. 'He has his problems, after all.'
She was terse and apparently dismissive.

'I don't want to interfere,' Robert said, with
little regard for truth. 'But I do think it might do
you no harm to talk this all out before you return
to London.'

'You have so many other things to think
about.'

'The entire evening for your problems, if you
think it would help you at all.'

'I broke my engagement, you know.' She was
abrupt.

'You did?' He tried to prevent the relief and
joy he experienced at the news from plastering
themselves right across his face. As a result he
succeeded in looking rather more forbidding than
usual.

Gabrielle concluded he was recollecting that
he'd told her the engagement was a mistake from
the beginning. 'I know you thought it was a mistake
anyway.'

He brushed this aside. 'You couldn't have
guessed this girl was going to surface. He hadn't
seen her for years, he told me himself.'

'Anyway, she's here now, and I've broken our
engagement off.'

'Very wise.'

'Whatever he says'—she made up her mind on
the spur of the moment—'it'll stay off until I've
sat the Membership again.'

'Good plan.' Robert poured more wine and
turned the conversation into a harmless discussion

about the most suitable books for intensive revision before taking the examination again in October.

'You do think I ought to try again as soon as that?'

'Certain of it. You'd have sailed through if you hadn't been upset.'

She glowed. Robert never praised lightly. 'Paul and Anik can get lost,' she promised him wildly. 'I'll put my head down and study, think of nothing else.' She smiled blindingly.

The waiter brought the cheese board.

While they were choosing, a plan began to form in Robert's mind. 'I might have an idea that could make matters a bit easier,' he said slowly. He cut a wedge of Stilton. 'David Paterson is thinking about the Membership too.'

Gabrielle knew David. A year junior to her, he was at present the resident house physician at Bramley House.

'He hopes to take it next year,' Robert was continuing. 'But he's a bit out of touch down here. Has plenty of time for revision, but he's not getting enough experience of teaching rounds and demonstrations or clinical meetings. Every month I come down he's on at me about it, asking if he could have a weekend relief so that he could at least come up to London for lectures on Saturdays. I've been dubious about it. Difficult to arrange, and he wouldn't gain all that much from the odd Saturday lecture or conference. But it occurs to me—how would you feel about relieving him for, say, three weeks or so?'

'Three weeks at Bramley House?'

'You don't particularly need more ward rounds. You're ready for the Membership, which he certainly isn't. But you'd have quiet evenings for revision, and you'd be out of the way. No interruptions from Paul.'

'Away from Paul and Anik.' The opportunity came like an answer to a prayer. 'Not part of any hideous tug of war.'

So that was how she thought of it. Robert would have enjoyed killing Paul, putting paid to his existence. All he said, however, was that in the morning he'd have a word with David Paterson. 'I'd suggest you and he might change over next Saturday.'

'I'd be very happy to do that.' She was formal, because once again Robert was very much the director of the unit, but she'd seldom felt more thankful. Three weeks of not seeing Paul. No longer would she be forced to meet him on ward rounds, do Outpatients with him, take part in case conferences, let alone constantly drink coffee with him in sister's office or run into him round any corner. No Paul for three weeks.

CHAPTER EIGHT

GABRIELLE travelled down to Bramley House earlier than had been originally planned—on Thursday morning. That afternoon she did a round with David Paterson, and the same evening he left for London and her own flat, which she was lending him for his stay. There was a weekend conference at the Institute for Child Health beginning on Friday afternoon, which he'd be able to catch before taking over at the Central on Monday morning.

Before her departure, existence was a rush. She had to write up her case notes, speak to sisters, social workers, family doctors as well as patients and their parents. She'd tidied up her flat ready for David, done her own packing and, finally and unnecessarily, hoovered and cleaned the flat. David wouldn't care. He'd very likely not even notice. But she owed it to herself, she felt, to leave the flat in good order.

All these preparations provided an excuse for not spending an evening with Paul. Too busy. Far too busy. Much too much to do. A frantic rush. Terribly sorry.

They'd said goodbye hastily in the corridor outside the ward.

'I shall miss you so much,' Paul said. 'But I

realise it's probably the right thing for you. I am afraid Anik's arrival has hit you hard.'

Gabrielle, with no regard whatsoever for truth, at once denied this hotly.

Paul shook his head. 'The director has been telling me I have not been considering you as I should.'

Gabrielle gaped. Robert had been telling Paul . . . ?

'I am afraid he is right. I have been thoughtless and self-centred. While you are away I shall see that Anik begins her training, and then I shall write to my parents and she will write to hers. After that you and I will be able to attend to our own affairs.'

Gabrielle found this prospect less enticing than she expected. 'We are not engaged, Paul,' she reminded him. 'Our future is an entirely separate issue from you and Anik. I am not, you see'—and she came out with it, the phrase that had surfaced when she was talking to Robert—'I refuse to be part of any tug of war.'

'But Gaby darling—'

'That's how I feel. Can't stay now. Sorry.' She turned and clattered away down the stairs.

This encounter, following a severe dressing down from Robert, demoralised Paul.

'What have you done about that girl from India, your fiancée?' Robert had asked him out of the blue on Monday, after they had finished discussing the week's admissions and discharges.

'Anik?' he asked, staring.

'Presumably. I imagine you have only the one fiancée from India?' Robert at his nastiest.

Paul gulped. 'Quite so, sir. She—er—she is at present staying with my uncle and aunt in Ledford.'

'Wasn't asking for her postal address. No intention of writing to her, I can assure you. What I want to know is, what have you done about her?'

'Done about her, sir? I met her at the airport, and—'

'What have you actually said to her about your engagement since her arrival? Have you explained your position?'

Paul looked uneasy. 'She knows I am not wanting to marry her.'

'Have you said so, since her arrival?'

Paul looked even less happy. 'It is not easy. I— after all, I could hardly greet her at Heathrow reminding her I wasn't wanting to marry her.'

'Perhaps not. But you should have made it clear by now. It's typical of you, Paul. The same with patients, aren't you? Don't you realise that, simply in order to spare yourself a little awkwardness, you're making two girls, neither of whom has any responsibility for the state of affairs other than to have agreed to marry you, utterly miserable?'

Paul made an attempt to interrupt, but Robert talked him down.

'Try looking at it in the simplest possible terms. Numerically. If you could bring yourself to hurt one of them, the other will be relieved of pain and stress. One unhappy girl where before there were two. Even the one you've hurt will at least know where she stands. Isn't that so?'

Reluctantly, Paul supposed it was.

'More than time you got a grip on the situation —for which, as I've just pointed out, you're solely responsible.'

'You are right, sir.' Paul sighed. 'I must face it, talk to Anik plainly.'

'What you ought to do is pack her straight off home.' It cost Robert a great deal to say this. He saw only too clearly that the result might be Gabrielle's marriage to Paul and her departure from the Central.

He need not have worried.

'Pack her off home?' Paul was horrified. 'I could never do that. In any case, Gabrielle is agreed with me that we mustn't do anything like that.'

'I daresay she is. She's a nice, well-meaning girl.' A nice, well-meaning girl. That was one way of putting it, but not the way he would have chosen. A beautiful, desirable, magical girl were the words that floated up instead. Hurriedly he pulled himself together. 'You ought not to have paid the slightest attention,' he barked. 'You ought to have gone straight ahead and done it. For Gabrielle's sake, if not your own.'

'Do you think I should?' Paul shook his head. 'Is too late now, I'm afraid. The hospital are expecting her for her course. She is committed to year's training. What I will do, however, at once—well, on my next free evening—is see her at Ledford. Tell her plainly that there can be no question of marriage, that she is here for her training. Nothing more.'

'Go this evening.'

'If I can find someone to stand in for me I will.'

Robert thought Paul might not try very hard to find anyone, and so be able to postpone any difficult confrontation. 'I'll take your calls,' he said. 'Tell Christopher to ring me if he's in any doubt, and you get straight off to Ledford.'

Since he was more than sceptical that Paul would, when it came to the point, nerve himself to speak honestly to Anik, he buttonholed him halfway through the week to check on the state of play. 'A word with you. In my office.'

'Sir?'

'Shut the door. Now, what have you done about that fiancée of yours?'

'I—I spoke to her, sir. She—she understands now that I mean what I say about our marriage.'

'*Now*! Didn't she before?'

'I—I'm afraid she seems to have imagined that —that I was dubious only about marrying a girl straight from India. She thought once she did her year's training here she would have shown me she was equipped for life in UK, and—and all would go ahead as planned.'

'Does she understand now?'

'She does. I—I took the plunge, and explained about my engagement to Gabrielle. Anik was very much upset. She said she would not have come to UK if she had known about it. I—I was wanting her to come up to London and meet Gabrielle—

I am sure this would help her. Gabrielle is so understanding. But now Gabrielle says she is leaving tomorrow for Bramley House. There is no time for meeting. Such a pity.'

This statement infuriated Robert. 'You ask far too much of Gabrielle. You're supposed to be a doctor, yet you can stand by and watch her tear herself apart because of you and your concerns. Apparently you notice nothing.'

'It is not easy for either of us.'

'I haven't seen you losing any weight. Gabrielle has. Not sleeping, either. Going round as if she's living through a nightmare. And she's failed the Membership.'

'But everyone fails the first time,' Paul protested.

'Everyone does not. You may have done. I didn't. And Gabrielle was expected to get it. However,' he ended unfairly, 'none of my business. Can't spend all day talking about your marital affairs. I'm going over to the surgical block for half an hour, and then I'll see you in the ward.' Almost knocking Paul over on his way to the door, he shouldered past him, and strode off down the corridor.

Half an hour later, at the same furious pace, leaping upstairs two or three steps at a time en route for his ward round, already overdue, he collided with Gabrielle, on her way down after saying goodbye to Paul.

'Sorry,' he snapped as he almost sent her flying. His arm fielded her securely, but then administered

an impatient and forceful shove in the opposite
direction. He longed to fold her into his arms and
stay there on the stairs for the rest of the afternoon,
but he was late for his round. In any case he dared
not stay and talk to her. Far too much could so
easily be said.

He rushed on upwards while Gabrielle plodded
down feeling amazingly upset. His abruptness
meant nothing, she reminded herself. He had a
reputation for never walking when he could run,
and he frequently gave registrars and housemen,
sisters and nurses, much as if they'd been his child
patients, a good hard shove in the direction they
were meant to follow. Even so, she was bereft.
She'd thought that they were at least on friendlier
terms now than this. She tried to put the unsatisfac-
tory encounter out of her mind, but she was sad
that this should have to be her last meeting with
him before she left.

At Bramley House, although her days were busy
and occupied, they were tranquil compared with
existence at the Central. Certainly they were not
quiet, since half the children were rampaging con-
valescents and full of cheek and exuberance. But
her evenings were her own, and then she hit the
books. As Robert had said, she'd done her stint of
ward rounds and seminars. What she needed was
to swot. And swot she did. All evening. Every
evening.

She refused to allow herself to brood on the
chaos of her personal affairs. It was all a muddle

and—again as Robert had pointed out—there could be no quick or easy solution. Down at Bramley House she could keep the future and its problems at bay, concentrate instead on looking after the children and on her revision. There were seldom any night calls, nor any rush to the wards to see a patient before breakfast. What she did do before the meal was to stroll along the lanes. Often she reached the stile where, in a fold of the downs, she could glimpse Robert's barn, its lichened roofs spread under the early morning sun. She thought about Robert far too much, she warned herself again and again.

Often, though, her thoughts were on neither Robert nor Paul, but on the children, her patients. She had an opportunity now to follow them up in much more detail than she could during hectic days at the Central.

It was an eye-opener.

She talked at length to the children themselves and to their parents when they visited. She noted family tensions and family strengths. She watched the children when they were not aware of her presence, and soon discovered that their behaviour could be entirely different if they supposed themselves unobserved. When they talked to her, they always presented what they imagined to be their best side. Obvious, once she'd spotted it. This after all, was how children were. Yet it had not occurred to her before.

Melanie, for instance, the little asthmatic from the night of her party, was down at Bramley

House for a month, for breathing exercises and investigations. Gabrielle watched her showing off and trying to patronise the other children—until one of them would turn on her and cut her down to size. But Melanie was resilient. She quickly moved towards someone different—a member of the staff, perhaps—and set herself to charm them instead, until she had successfully established herself again in the centre of her own small stage. It was when Melanie was edged from the centre that, plainly, her own little world collapsed and she couldn't cope. So was this, Gabrielle began to wonder, the explanation for her asthmatic attacks? Was it when her father was at home and she had to compete for a share of the limelight, that she perhaps tried too hard and too long, and finally succumbed to another attack? These attacks always, inevitably, brought her the attention she craved—though at what a price.

Gabrielle promised herself a long talk with Mrs Tower, Melanie's mother, when she next visited her daughter. Before that, however, she was due for a weekend off, and had arranged to spend it with Nicola and Andrew.

On Thursday, though, Paul rang her, to inform her that Anik's first post at the Central was to be at Bramley House.

'I see.' Gabrielle was nonplussed.

'So I am driving her down on Saturday morning. I thought we might have lunch together. That would be pleasant arrangement. Nice for Anik to meet you before she goes on duty in the wards, I am thinking.'

Nice for Anik, indeed. All Gabrielle's hard-won composure shattered. Anik, there with her at Bramley House. So much for her peace and tranquillity. One thing was certain, though. Gabrielle set her lips. No way was she going to cancel her weekend for either Paul or Anik. Not at any price. 'I shan't be here. I'm spending the weekend with Nicola and Andrew. I go tomorrow evening, and I can't possibly cancel at this stage.' What's more, I wouldn't if I could.

Paul was much more put out than he allowed her to guess. He'd seen Anik's appointment to Bramley House as a useful opportunity to get in touch with Gabrielle in spite of her embargo. Now, disappointed—unnerved, too, by her apparent coolness—he mumbled a few remarks about it being a pity, another time, perhaps. 'My best regards to Nicola and Andrew,' he ended, putting a brave face on the inevitable.

Unluckily for him, this finality annoyed Gabrielle almost as much as anything that had gone before. 'My regards to Anik,' she responded frigidly. They sounded, she and Paul, like a couple of superannuated pundits exchanging compliments on a doorstep in Harley Street, she thought crossly as she put the telephone down.

And then the real impact of his news hit her again. That was all she needed. For the rest of her stay, she'd have to meet Anik daily. Not only in the wards, either, but in the dining room. At

Bramley House there was only one staff dining room. An old-fashioned dining room, too, with one long table for residents, the resident medical officer—Gabrielle—at one end, the sister-in-charge at the other, the remainder of the staff ranged between them. Every meal at the same table as Anik.

'So much for forgetting all my problems,' she complained bitterly to Nicola, minutes after her arrival.

'You must try and treat it as an opportunity,' Nicola retorted unsympathetically. 'Anyway, you can't pretend it's anything to do with Paul.'

Gabrielle scowled. She intended to go on blaming Paul. It was easy to release all her hidden anger with him, stored up as problems mounted through the weeks, on this one outrageous incident.

'Not Paul at all,' Nicola pointed out. 'Simply the chief nursing officer being kind, for once, to a newcomer.'

The reiteration of this obvious truth deepened Gabrielle's scowl.

'Don't be silly,' Nicola went on, patting her son to bring his wind up, and gazing calmly past his dark head to Gabrielle's glum expression. 'There's nothing Paul could have done about it, as you know perfectly well. Entirely a matter for the nursing staff. And at least he rang you up and told you. So what's got into you? You're being terribly unfair. Are you jealous of Anik, is that it?'

Gabrielle sighed, and shook her head. 'I simply have no idea. I don't know what's got into me, what I feel or why. This trouble over Paul and Anik seems to bring out all kinds of emotions I didn't know I possessed. But what I really feel—I haven't a clue.'

'Part of your problem is you're not used to being in love. Me, I can tell you, I've been through it again and again, and there's no love without mood swings. Up in the clouds, down in the depths.'

'But I didn't think it would be like that with Paul, you see. I thought he was so safe.'

Nicola's eyebrows climbed up into her blonde fringe. 'You were bound to be wrong about that, you know.'

'But why?'

'No one is that safe. Though I do agree you've been incredibly unlucky. Although personally, I think, now it's happened, you might find it's very useful to have Anik down at Bramley House.'

'*Useful*?' Gabrielle screeched. 'You must be out of your tiny mind. How can Anik being there possibly be useful?'

'While Paul's out of the way, you'll be able to get to know each other. Work out where you both stand, what you both want.'

This programme failed to enthral Gabrielle. 'Just as I thought I was getting on top of the situation at last, bang, this. One telephone call from Paul and I'm back where I started.'

Nicola frowned. 'Poor love, you are in a bit of a bad way, aren't you? There's no doubt you've had a raw deal. In fact, if I didn't know Paul, what he's like and how kind he is, so that I understand exactly how he's got both of you into this spot, I'd say he'd let you down badly. I can see it's hell for you.'

'More hell than I ever expected,' Gabrielle admitted. 'Something I never supposed I'd have to face with anyone like Paul.'

'Well, you do have to. So what do you feel about him?'

'I simply don't know.'

'Do you still love him in spite of everything?'

Did she? Uncertainly, Gabrielle shook her head. 'If only I knew that I'd know where I stood.'

'Part of your trouble is that you had a different existence from the rest of us when we were students, you know. Having the responsibility for your grandmother like that, looking after her, always knowing at the back of your mind that there was no hope, that it could only end the way it finally did. After that you had to set to and sell your old home, too, and there you were on your own.'

For the first time Gabrielle smiled. 'Not on my own,' she said. 'I had you. You were terrific. You were trying to qualify, too. But you helped me clear out the house and look for a flat—and then you moved in and shared it with me. I don't think I could have coped without you. And you were just starting up with Andrew, too—you could easily have forgotten everyone except him. But you didn't.'

'Ah, but that's exactly what I'm on about. I had Andrew. You had no one. You'd been far too busy, as well as too cut off, going home every day to Stanmore. Paul is the first man in your life. You're inexperienced, love.' She grinned. 'True, you know. And I don't honestly think—you may not like this—I don't think it's a good idea to spend the rest of your life with the first man you fall for. What's more, with Paul, I don't think it would work, if you give up everything to go to Ledford with him. I was going to say that to you anyway, even if none of this had happened.'

'I'm a bit dubious myself about that,' Gabrielle was forced to admit. 'But—'

'You didn't choose Paul for himself at all, I'm sure of it. You mixed him up with all sorts of other things. All right, it might have worked. Or it might not. But it wasn't terribly likely to have come off, I don't think. And you can't tell me you were exactly swept off your feet with passion, can you?'

'No. It wasn't like that at all. But there was so much that drew me to him. Thoughtfulness and kindness and—and—' her voice trailed off into silence as she saw Nicola's expression.

'Security, he offered. But it's not enough, Gaby. Not for marriage. Marriage is for a lifetime. And it's disastrous to go looking for it, anyway. It ought to hit you so that you can't get away, and go on hitting you. Oh, you were due for somebody like Paul. You needed him. For a while. Not for the remainder of your days. I'm pretty sure, you know, if you'd gone ahead and married him, and lived that life you thought you were so mad about, you'd soon have got bored to extinction with it. It's very easy, don't we all know, to fall for someone senior who helps you when you're new and raw. If he happens also to be good-looking and incredibly kind, like Paul—right, you're swept off your feet. But you don't have to marry the bloke.'

'Look, I—'

'What's more, if you did—marry Paul, I mean —you'd soon be missing the Central, wishing you had opted for a registrar's post there instead, where it's all happening.'

'You sound exactly like Robert Scorer,' Gabrielle said disgustedly. 'That's the line he keeps ramming down my throat.'

'There you are, you see. I'm not the only one.'

'Oh no, you're not the only one.'

'Listen, whoever you marry, there are going to be days, weeks probably, when you ask yourself what the hell you've got into, and why. I do. When Andrew's called out, and here I am, another evening on my own with only junior to make faces at.' She stuck her tongue out at the carry-cot at her side. 'Or when Andrew's tired and fed up and unsociable, and here I am, longing to be stimulated and taken out of myself for a change. Marriage isn't one long dream of heady bliss. So don't rush into it. I didn't marry Andrew because I wanted to live in this hole and keep house and have babies. I married him because I couldn't bloody live without him.'

'I thought I felt like that about Paul,' Gabrielle said unhappily.

'But now you're not sure. If you ask me, Anik

may have done you a good turn, arriving like this. Given you a chance to think. To reconsider.'

'Great. Thanks very much.' Gabrielle was angrily sarcastic, but the next day, trundling back to Bramley House in the slow train, she saw what Nicola meant and had to admit to herself that she might even be right. A great deal to which she'd been blind—for years, almost—fell neatly into place, and as the train rattled on, stopping and starting at small country stations, she stared across the fields and wondered why it had taken her so long to understand what now seemed so plain.

She had turned to Paul for security, not for love. Because he offered so much kindness, with a ready-made home waiting, too, attached to his uncle's practice. Marry Paul, an inner voice must have told her, and there you are with a home and a family again.

Relax back into the womb, she commented scornfully now. Leave the Central and all its challenge, retrace your steps back into the family life that had been snatched away when Gran died.

So naturally, when what Paul was offering in fact proved to be the reverse of security, she was thrown.

If only Gran hadn't died. The longing jolted her into yet another new understanding. If Gran hadn't died, none of this would have happened. She would never have thought of getting engaged to Paul.

The memory of Gran brought more affection than pain now, and Gabrielle went on thinking about her, dreaming about their old home, and Gran's little sayings. Her hard work, too. She was the one who had kept the family together, who had given Gabrielle her happy childhood.

She must have been crazy, she decided, to imagine that any new set-up could replace the home Gran had provided. She should have given herself time to heal. Instead she had rushed into marriage with Paul and admission to his family circle. Serve her right if the whole scheme had backfired on her. She ought to be thankful.

Robert had been right from the beginning. Marriage to Paul and life in Ledford would never have worked for her. All she had to make sure about now was that in extricating herself from it she would not hurt Paul too much. He had tried always to do his best for her, and he deserved her gentleness and understanding—which were only, after all, the qualities he had offered her, and which she had at one time so much valued.

What she had to do was absolutely clear at last. It was also, maddeningly, what Robert had told her from the beginning. She had to get the Membership, followed by a registrar's post at the Central.

That would give her time. Time to find out what she really felt for Paul, apart from his family and the Ledford practice. Time to find out if, as Nicola had said, she loved him enough to give up the Central and her career because she couldn't live without him. They'd have two years apart. He could sort out the problem of Anik, and she could discover whether she missed him enough to marry him.

She could also, a small but unheeded voice reminded her, discover what she was going to do about Robert.

CHAPTER NINE

AT BREAKFAST on Monday morning, there unmistakably was Anik, wearing a staff nurse's print and a flyaway cap over dark hair drawn back from an oval face. No escaping it, she was beautiful.

Whether by accident or design, she was sitting at the far end of the table, and left the dining-room with a group of nurses going on duty while Gabrielle was still eating toast and marmalade.

At lunch the room was crowded, with the non-residents' tables occupied and a constant coming and going. Anik was in the same position at the far end of the big table, Gabrielle saw, and she paused, wondering whether to walk straight over to Anik to greet her and tell her she'd been sorry to miss her on Saturday. Her brief pause, though, allowed the physiotherapist who had been trailing her down the corridor to catch her.

'I wanted to have a word about Melanie Tower, if you can spare a moment,' she said. 'I was wondering if we could make a date? For the last few days Melanie hasn't bothered to try much with her breathing exercises, but I rather think, given an audience, she'll get cracking again. A thorough little show-off, that one—like her parents, of course. Not her fault really.'

Gabrielle was puzzled. 'Her mother, perhaps.

But surely not her father? A quiet, unassertive man, he seemed to me.'

'Clearly you haven't seen Melanie's latest photograph.'

In important frames, Melanie's photographs stood on her locker, showing Mr and Mrs Tower looking very grand at their wedding, almost equally grand at Melanie's christening, and with their daughter in a studio portrait.

'The christening photograph has been removed,' the physiotherapist was explaining. 'The latest arrival shows Mr and Mrs Tower more stunning then ever, winning a ballroom dancing contest.'

The new photograph stood in front of the other two, and displayed Mr Tower, handsome in full evening dress with tails, twirling Mrs Tower in a frilly tulle gown with a sequined bodice.

'What a super photograph,' Gabrielle said. 'I didn't know your parents went in for ballroom dancing.'

'They don't now. Not since they had me.' Melanie was smug.

'You mean they've given it up?'

Melanie nodded. She looked rather pleased with herself, Gabrielle thought, and the next afternoon when Mrs Tower came to visit Melanie, Gabrielle took her off into the office for a quiet chat. 'I gather you used to do a lot of ballroom dancing, but that you don't any more,' she began. 'It seems such a pity, when you were so good. You must have enjoyed it so much.'

Mrs Tower shrugged. 'Can't leave Melanie, can we?'

'Surely, though—I can see it would have been difficult while she was a baby, but she's old enough by now to be left with a good baby-sitter occasionally, surely?'

'You sound just like my husband.' The words erupted violently, carrying a load of hostility.

Gabrielle was taken by surprise, but she persevered. 'He says that? But you don't agree? You feel she can't be left, do you?'

'I'm not prepared to risk her having an attack, just so that we can go dancing, no.' Mrs Tower was definite.

'Melanie doesn't like the two of you to go off, is that it, and leave her behind?'

'It upsets her.' Mrs Tower was short.

'I see. And then she gets asthma, is that it?'

'Well, what do you suppose, Doctor?'

Mrs Tower was plainly hostile, and Gabrielle decided to leave the question alone for the time being. At the weekend, when both parents were down, she'd try again.

Already nearly half the week had gone, and she had made no contact with Anik, she realised. They must meet and have a talk—and without interruptions—she thought. Although she wasn't keen to spare an evening in the middle of her revision, she came to the conclusion there was nothing else for it, and left a note for Anik in the letter rack in the hall, inviting her to a meal in Southbridge on her next free evening.

Anik rang her in the office. 'This is being so kind of you,' a soft voice said. 'Are you sure it is what you want?'

'Yes, of course. When are you free?'

'On Thursday I am off from five o'clock, so I could meet you at any time you say.'

'How about catching the six-thirty bus at the gate, then? We could go into Southbridge and have a meal at the Rose & Crown.'

'It is very kind of you. I would like that very much.'

'I look forward to it.' Hardly the truth, Gabrielle thought. In fact, she dreaded the evening. Very likely Anik did too.

Whether she did or not, she was there at the bus stop on time, out of uniform and looking as beautiful as ever in a pretty flowery sari with a tweed coat over it. They smiled strained smiles at one another, climbed on to the bus and chatted uneasily about the road to Southbridge and the Rose & Crown's meals, descended from the bus in the market square and walked across to the hotel.

They settled down in the lounge, while Gabrielle ordered orange juice for Anik and vermouth for herself.

'Is nice here,' Anik said politely. 'Is indeed good of you to spend an evening with newly-arrived staff nurse. For you are important person here in Bramley House, I see for myself. On the ward they are most impressed I am coming out to meal with you. My stock has gone up.' Seated in a low arm-chair in her silk sari, her dark hair drawn back from aquiline features, her eyes huge and brown, she smiled with apparently genuine amusement. She had a lovely smile, a shade wistful but charmingly endearing, and a soft melodious voice.

Gabrielle flushed, began a sentence disclaiming any importance anywhere, and then cut through her own flounderings with a determination they would have recognised on the wards. 'I thought we owed ourselves a quiet talk about Paul, away from all those flapping ears and eyes on stalks. Tell me, how did you get on with Paul's uncle and aunt?'

'They were so very helpful. His Aunt Debi took me shopping for clothes for the winter—this coat, she advised me to buy. And some shoes for muddy lanes, and warm gloves. Also a woolly hat and a scarf. I am now well equipped.' She smiled her lovely smile again.

These were polite nothings, when they had met —at least as far as Gabrielle was concerned—with the purpose of being honest with one another. 'Down to brass tacks,' she said firmly, though with inner qualms. 'How did you and Paul get on?'

For the first time, Anik evaded her eyes. 'He is being so kind.'

Gabrielle was determined not to be put off like this all evening. 'I'm sure. He is kind. But what do you feel about him, now you've met him again?'

Anik fidgeted with the edge of her sari, rolling it up and unrolling it with nervous fingers. 'I am not knowing what I feel at all. There has been no time for finding out. All is so new, and different. But what I must say to you, with no doubt at all, is how grateful I am being, to you even more than to Paul, for saying nothing to my parents or his. For giving me opportunity to come to UK for this year. Is as much difficult for you as for me, I see that.'

She could say that again, Gabrielle thought, with a momentary touch of bitterness. Somehow, though, if their meeting tonight was to be at all worth while, she had to cut through Anik's courteous politeness and discover the girl inside. 'I'm sorry, Anik, if I seem interfering, but do please stop being so polite. Don't you see, if you and I can't be truthful with one another, we're going to find ourselves stuck in the most horrible muddle, on and on.'

'Horrible muddle is undoubtedly what I am in, though I am trying to find way through. But it is, you see, step by step, and I must say I do not know at all where I am or what I am going to feel next week or next month. In year's time I have to go back home, everyone knowing there is to be no marriage. This I cannot imagine at present, but in twelve months perhaps all will have changed. I shall be different person, I shall not mind any longer. So I am hoping.'

'Listen, Anik, we have to work out the future together. All three of us. You and I and Paul. But mostly you and I. Because Paul is the one in the middle. He doesn't know which way to turn.'

'But you are wrong, Gabrielle. He knows very well. He has turned to you. It is I who am interloper.'

Gabrielle shoook her head. 'He told you I broke off our engagement?'

'On account of me, yes. But is only formality, he told me.'

'That's what I want to explain. One of the things I want to explain. It's more than just a form of words. It's real. It may have been a formality at first, but it's become true. After I broke off the engagement I changed. I no longer, somehow, felt engaged to him any more.'

'That I understand very well. Is how I too feel. Is different, entirely, from being affianced. Is not very nice. But I get used to it.'

'Me, too. Especially when I came down here and stopped seeing Paul any more. I found I was able to work things out a bit. And I decided that instead of joining Paul in Ledford this year as we'd planned, I must do what everyone at the hospital said all along I ought to do, try for a registrar's post at the Central. People say I ought to get it, and if I do, it will mean two more years in London. Also two years of general practice in Ledford for Paul, without me. So this is what I'm going to tell him. We have two years apart, and only after that do we think about any future together. I thought you ought to know. It affects you, too.'

'Is this what you want to do, Gabrielle, I must ask? Or what you think you ought to do? On account of me.'

'It arose because of you in the first place. But

it's become what I truly want to do. I've found out that I don't want to miss the next two years at the Central.'

'I have only the one year. After that I will be gone, I promise you. After that I return and face the future. I must tell you, Gabrielle, at first when Paul told me about you, I am angry. I say to him he ought to have told me this before I left home. Because when I decided to come to UK, it was to show him I am not unsuitable as wife—you see, I am supposing still that is why he wants to cancel marriage. Because I know nothing of UK life. If I had known then he is wanting to marry you, I would never have come.'

'But Paul and I both wanted you to come, to take up your chance of training here.'

'That is what he tell me, again and again. That you want me to have my training here as planned. I see now it is true. You and Paul, you have given me this year, and I am determined to make use of it. Already I am better equipped for future, no longer am I provincial Indian girl. I will return different person. I am learning to be independent.'

'You know, you're saying exactly what I've been thinking myself. You and I must both become independent, so that Paul is responsible for neither of us.'

Their eyes met. Anik nodded soberly. 'You are right, yes. In these days, not like old traditional days, a girl like myself should no longer think of marrying until she has learnt independence, it seems to me. Is no longer good thing at all to go straight from father's house to husband's. One should stand on own two feet first.'

That about summed it up, Gabrielle thought. Anik had seen it clearly. Gabrielle's mistake had been to try to make Paul a substitute for her lost family and home, when she ought to have been learning, exactly as Anik said, to stand on her own feet.

Right. It was settled. At the end of the following week she would return to London and tell Paul she was going to do another two years at the Central. After that they could, if they still wanted to, think about their future.

What if, long before that, he had married Anik?

The future must take care of itself. Her decision, she was sure, was the right one today. What it might lead to for any of the three of them was impossible to foretell. And now she must push these difficulties to the back of her mind. Because next weekend had not arrived. She had this weekend and its problems to deal with, and one of these was to talk to Melanie's father.

Here, at last, she struck gold.

'No,' he agreed angrily, sitting opposite her in the little office. 'No more bloody dancing. And all because of young Melanie.' He thumped the desk top with a furious fist. 'It's not right, Doctor. You can't tell me it is, because I know in my bones it's wrong. But can I get Susie to see it?'

'I suppose it might upset Melanie—'

'Might? Does, you mean. If there's so much as

a hint we might be planning to go dancing, she's straight into one of her attacks. So Susie says we must just give up our dancing—but you can't tell me that's the right way to tackle it. After all, Melanie has to grow up into the real world and come to terms with life as it is, not as she wants it to be. She's got to accept facts.'

'I expect she's frightened, when you go off together and she's left behind, and that's what triggers the attack.'

'She knows we'll be back. She just likes her own way, and she's found out how to make sure she gets it. Only her mother won't see it. Gives into her right along the line.'

'You mustn't feel that Melanie actually, so to speak, manufactures an attack, Mr Tower. What probably happens is that she does get frightened, for whatever reason, and that produces the attack.'

'She can't be afraid of losing me and Susie, just because we go dancing together once a week. It looks to me much more like temper.'

He had something there, Gabrielle had to admit. 'Melanie likes the centre of the stage,' she said slowly. 'We've all seen that. And probably she gets frightened if she sees you putting her in second place.'

'She can't go through life like that, Doctor. But me and Susie, we don't know how to deal with it, and that's a fact. Because once she does get an attack, poor little beggar, it takes hell out of her. When it gets to that point, I'm the same as Susie, I'll do anything just so long as she gets better.'

Melanie had her parents in a double-bind, and Gabrielle guessed that somewhere in her depths she knew it and traded on it. But her father was right. For her own sake Melanie had to learn to rely on herself, instead of blackmailing her family.

Momentarily, as Gabrielle sat in her office in Bramley House, she ached for Robert. If only he could appear miraculously by her side, and find a way—as he would, she was certain—to solve this problem for her.

She pressed her lips together. She was as bad as Melanie, yearning for outside support. She had to pull herself together. She was trained, and Melanie was in her care. What was more, step by step she was making progress. At least she understood now what caused the weekend attacks. And then, out of the blue, in a flash of intuition, a possible method of dealing with the situation opened out before her.

'Mr Tower, have you ever thought of encouraging Melanie to take up ballroom dancing too?'

His eyes popped. 'Melanie? With her asthma? How could she?'

'She could try. And it might be the best thing for her.' A line of treatment that, if it worked, could change Melanie's entire life. She began to explain it to Mr Tower. 'She's doing breathing exercises now,' she said. 'If she can master them, they'll not only be good for her chest, they could help her to control her asthmatic attacks. But she soon gets bored with the exercises, and she's not really trying very hard.'

Mr Tower sighed. 'That's my Melanie,' he said sadly.

'So how about suggesting that when she's good enough at them you'll enrol her in ballroom dancing classes?'

'Doctor, you're right. It could work.'

'Once she starts them, then you could dangle in front of her the chance of going dancing with you both, as soon as she's good enough. You might sometimes practise with her.'

Mr Tower stared at her as if she'd offered him heaven on a plate. 'Doctor, if it came off—and you're right, it easily could—it would change our lives. I've sometimes wondered how I'm going to go on like this, Susie and Melanie playing into one another's hands the way they do, and no end to it. If it works, this plan, it wouldn't just give Melanie a proper future, it would change all our lives.'

'Let's give it a try, then, shall we? You explain it to your wife, will you?'

'I'll certainly do that, Doctor. And thank you for everything.' A spring in his step, he went out of the office and off to join his family.

Gabrielle sat on in the empty office. She was elated. Through her efforts, a new life might be opening for three people.

Her hand reached out for the telephone.

She snatched it back hastily. For a mad moment she'd been going to ring Robert to share her hopes for the Tower family with him. She must be losing her marbles. The director would be furious to be disturbed on a Sunday morning, at home in that flat of his, by a junior doctor gabbling about breathing exercises and ballroom dancing classes for one of the asthmatic children at Bramley House.

It was the middle of the following week before he rang her, saying he wanted her to remain at Bramley House for a further two weeks, to allow David Paterson to fit in his annual leave before returning. Would she mind?

'No, of course not.' What else could she say?

'I'll be down this Saturday as usual, so I'll see you then. Any problems that can't wait?'

She could hardly tell him about Melanie now, he'd snap her head off. 'I don't think so, thank you.'

'Good. Make sure everything's ready for me, won't you? Many thanks.' The line went dead.

Gabrielle glared at the telephone on her desk as if it had just bitten her. What did he imagine she'd do, left to herself? Not bother? Say nothing to the staff about either the clinic or the ward round until it was on them? Meet him without the faintest idea of what was in the case papers, no notion of any patient's history? Angry and bitterly disappointed, she told herself Robert Scorer was impossible.

Irritated into detailed perfectionism, she checked the case histories of all the children due to attend the monthly clinic, nagged the ward staff about all their patients, and went out of her way to prepare for every unlikely contingency. Finally, on Saturday morning, coolly poised and groomed from the crown of her shining dark head to the tips of her highly polished classic court shoes, she greeted him at the door with stiff and formal courtesy.

In spite of this inauspicous start the clinic, to her immense relief, went like a dream. Afterwards they had lunch together in the dining room, during which she was at last able to tell him about the Tower family, and then embarked on the ward round. In the medical ward Anik was in charge, impeccable in the candy stripes of a staff nurse and with a crisp and gleaming apron newly donned for the occasion.

'I don't think you know Staff Nurse Rao,' Gabrielle began. 'She has just joined us from India. She's—er—' she stopped, at a loss. She'd been about to say Dr Singh's fiancée, but that would hardly do. Embarrassing for Anik, even if Robert, as she was reasonably certain he would, took it in his stride. 'She's been staying with Dr Singh's uncle and aunt in Ledford,' she substituted, and saw from a gleam in Robert's eye that he was fully aware of her predicament.

He gave nothing away, though, nodding pleasantly enough to Anik, saying he hoped she'd enjoy her stay, and how did she find the English weather?

Anik found it no colder than she'd been led to expect, and was wondering whether she'd see any snow here in the country. The children had been telling her there would be snow for Christmas.

'They hope,' Robert added.

A chorus of children promptly informed him there was *always* snow for Christmas, and tobogganing, and a snow man on the front lawn.

'And snowball fights. You want to watch out, Staff. They're demons with snowballs, these kids.'

'Snowballs?' Anik was puzzled.

The ward enlightened her.

Plainly, as far as the ward was concerned, Anik had made the grade, and they had taken her to their hearts. Gabrielle was a favourite too, and Robert they all adored, so it was to a clamour of cheeky and ecstatic yells that, half an hour later, Robert and Gabrielle departed.

This had been the final ward on the afternoon round, and as they descended the stairs towards the office and tea, Robert remarked amiably, 'So that's your rival, is it?'

'There's no question of a rival.' Gabrielle would have liked to hit him. 'In any case, as I've explained before, Paul and I are no longer engaged. Anik is —is—'

'Is what? Still engaged?' He was silky.

'Well, yes, in a way. She hasn't yet told her parents that the engagement is ended. We thought that—that it would be better to let her get thoroughly settled in before—before—well, stirring up trouble at home for her.'

'I see. "We" consisting of whom?'

They were in the office now, but they might as well have been on a ward round, and a very nasty one at that, Gabrielle thought resentfully. 'Of all three of us,' she said stiffly, and started to pour the tea. She handed him his cup, her eyes sparking fire.

'Thank you,' he said affably. 'Nice to see you've

joined the land of the living once more.' He bit
into a ginger nut.

Gabrielle refused to understand him. 'I don't
know what you mean.'

'Come on.' He grinned cheerfully. 'You've
never been slow in the uptake.'

Gabrielle, glowering, sipped her tea.

Glinting dark eyes probed, unconcealed laughter in their depths.

Not for the first time, Gabrielle had to give in.
'I do feel a lot more human and able to cope than
when I came down here,' she admitted. 'Thank
you for thinking of it.'

'Something had to be done,' he said brusquely.
'Any more tea?'

'Of course.' She took his cup, poured, and
returned it to him.

He received it absent-mindedly, his eyes on the
case history he'd begun reading. Presumably,
having dealt satisfactorily with her problems, he'd
returned to his real interest, the children in the
wards. After all, Gabrielle reminded herself, that
was what they were there for. Even so, she experienced a distinct sense of disappointment.

For over an hour they went through each case
in Bramley House, deciding on management, drug
regimes, diet, physiotherapy, and fixing admissions
and discharges. Finally Robert stretched, and
smiled at her. 'That seems to be that,' he said. 'Not
a bad day's work, eh?'

'Even quite good, perhaps?' She smiled back at
him.

'So how about a bit of relaxation? Care to come out for a meal this evening?'

More than she deserved, Gabrielle realised, accepting with surprised delight.

'Good. Right. I want to see to one or two oddments at the barn first—how about if I call for you here about seven-thirty, say?'

'I'll be ready.'

Gabrielle went out to the forecourt, as a good junior resident should, to see him into his car, and watched him turn out of the drive and disappear along the lane. She longed to be sitting next to him, joining him in the barn under the raftered roof, perhaps sitting with him in front of the wood stove in the early autumn twilight. Irritably she twitched narrow shoulders. She was being incredibly silly. She was going out for a meal with him in any case, in—she glanced at her watch—in less than an hour and a half. What she ought to do was beat it back into the office fast, write up the treatments, get the case papers back into order and into the filing cabinet. After that, with luck, she just might have time for a shower before she changed.

What to wear?

Her best beige silk might be overdoing it. The sole alternative was her grey corduroy skirt and waistcoat. That would have to do. Fortunately she had a new ruffled blouse she'd recently bought in a little boutique in Southbridge.

For God's sake stop fussing like a wet hen, she snapped at herself furiously. All she had to do, after all, was appear neat and tidy, a correct young doctor out with her chief after a busy day. It happened all the time. So what was she getting so steamed up about?

She brushed her hair out and let it hang round lavender chiffon shoulders, sprayed herself—oh, treachery—with the *Rive Gauche* Paul had given her for her birthday, fastened Gran's amethyst brooch at her throat, and nodded at her reflection. 'You'll do.' She picked up Gran's lacy Shetland shawl that had suddenly jumped into high fashion, and descended to the hall in time to see Robert turning into the drive, pulling up by the front door. A sense of excitement suffused her and the evening air filled with promise.

Had she only been able to see into his soul, she would have found Robert's emotions almost the same. As he had driven back to the barn after their day together, his heart sang, radiant with inexplicable joy.

He had informed himself severely that his mood was not only irrational but ludicrous, had walked briskly through the raftered room—chilly in the autumn evening—into the little bedroom Gabrielle had occupied, switched on the electric fire and settled down to go through his own paper and the outline programme for the next day, a Sunday consultants' conference which he was chairing at the hospital. His eyes followed the lines of typescript that constituted his paper opening the meeting, but his inner eyes were with a slender dark girl, her hair knotted at the base of her neck, who had accompanied him throughout his day, somehow making each hour a dream of joy.

He must be out of his mind.

If only he didn't have this wretched conference in London tomorrow, Gabrielle could be with him here all weekend. He would have fetched in wood, lighted the stove, and they could have sat by it together. They would cook their meals in the kitchen, and—

He had no more than a jar of Nescafé and a pound of apples in the place. Never mind.

They would have sat together by the·flickering flames, in the air scented by burning wood, he would have taken his beautiful, fantastic Gabrielle into his arms, undressed her by the fire, and made love to her. All night. All day. And all night again.

He shook his head, and made a determined effort to return to the typescript in his hand.

Undoubtedly Gabrielle was looking much better than she had done in London. He'd been right to send her down to Bramley House, right to arrange that extra fortnight there for her. Much wiser not to have her back into the Central until Paul had left for Ledford. If he was around to keep on upsetting her, all the good work would be wasted. Bad enough, in any case, that the Indian girl was here with Gabrielle at Bramley House. It had failed to cross his mind that they might send her out to the country for the first months of her training. He'd slipped up there. His error.

'You've boobed, Scorer.'

He shook his head. Alone in the barn, muttering

away to himself, and all because of a dark slip of a girl who'd failed the Membership when she ought to have passed, and who was in love with an excessively ordinary young registrar going into general practice. Paul was a good type, nothing wrong with him, except he was not worthy of Gabrielle.

Not worthy of Gabrielle.

How Victorian could he get?

What he had to do was pull himself together, wipe away these boy's dreams, and take Gabrielle out to dinner, behaving as if she were yet another junior he was feeding after a busy day. He'd done it often enough. There was nothing unusual about this evening. Nothing whatsoever.

Yet as he turned into the drive at Bramley House, he saw the pleasant but ordinary red brick porch, the tall sash windows, the gravel drive, all at once take on the excitement of a Covent Garden set as the curtain rose. Magic was everywhere. Life would never be the same again.

Out of the front door stepped Gabrielle. His Gabrielle. More beautiful than he'd ever seen her in some sort of grey outfit with a misty blue shawl that wrapped her round like a cloud.

Much more like a ravished boy than her confident chief, Robert fell out of the car and rushed round to open the door for her, devouring her with his eyes as he came.

Gabrielle could hardly fail to be scorched by him. She caught her breath. This was what she'd been waiting for all her life. For Robert to look at her like that.

CHAPTER TEN

As THEY drove through narrow, twisting lanes up into the downs, inhibition took hold of both of them.

'The colours are gorgeous round here,' Gabrielle volunteered tritely. 'I love autumn.'

'I like beechwoods at any time of year, but I must admit they're pretty spectacular now,' Robert rejoined. He frowned intimidatingly.

Gabrielle was duly intimidated, and decided she must have imagined his earlier look.

Robert reminded himself that the beauty of the beeches was a far safer subject than the beauty of Gabrielle herself. Enough that he had her there, warm and pulsing in the car alongside him. For a few hours he had her to himself. That must be all. He reminded himself sternly—frowning even more alarmingly—that he'd sent her down to Bramley House to recover from the unhappiness and turmoil she'd been through with Paul. He'd sent her there, in fact, to give her time and opportunity to get back to normal. He mustn't attempt to start something new. Not yet. The last thing she could possibly want was to be plunged headlong into a new relationship before she'd extricated herself from the old. If, that was, she had any intention of extricating herself.

The car nosed its way up a tortuous chalky lane between high hedges, round another corner, and they had arrived in a quiet, winding village street high up in the downs. A small upland village, a few scattered houses, two farms and a pub, called, unsurprisingly, the Plough.

'This is it. Doesn't look up to much, but the food's astonishing.'

'But it's charming,' Gabrielle told him politely.

This was to exaggerate. The little pub was hardly more than ordinary. Red brick, two-storeyed, with small casement windows of no particular period, only the steeply pitched roof of mellow red tiles had any claim to charm. The place was well cared for. The paint white and gleaming, the brass shining, a white-painted seat outside the door, tubs of plants in the paved forecourt already planted for winter with conifers, aucuba and variegated ivy.

'This way,' Robert said, leading her in and along a narrow passage past doors to the public bar and the saloon bar, a roar of voices coming from each. He opened another door, and ushered her into a small, square, low-ceilinged dining-room crowded with tables and apparently fully occupied. His eyes, though, searched and spotted a table for two on the far side of the room. 'There we are, I think,' he said. 'To the right of the fireplace.'

They crossed the room and sat down. Gabrielle looked about her. Someone had taken trouble, and the room, though as unpretentious as the outside of the house, was attractive and welcoming, with terracotta tablecloths and curtains, pale green walls, and pale green china on each table. The floor was quarry-tiled, and the chairs wheel-back. She smiled at Robert. 'Nice,' she said.

His heart turned over. All he said was 'Not much variety in the way of food, I'm afraid. What there is will almost certainly be delicious, but there'll be one dish of the day and that's it.'

A cheerful middle-aged lady in a flowery overall appeared at his side.

'Hullo, Mrs Walpole,' he said at once. 'How are you?'

'Very well, Doctor, thank you. Nice to see you again—quite some time since you've been in.'

'Yes, well, I'm based in London now, you know, and I don't get down here nearly as often as I'd like. This is Dr Vereker, who's working at Bramley House for a while. I've brought her along to sample your cooking. So what are you giving us tonight?'

'Steak-and-kidney pie with oysters and mushrooms. All right?'

'Very much so. And for you, Gaby?'

He'd called her Gaby again. 'Sounds marvellous,' she said coolly, and smiled at Mrs Walpole with her heart in her eyes, considerably startling that lady.

Robert, though, studying the handwritten menu, failed to catch the look, and said only, 'Smoked trout do you to start?'

'Great.' Gabrielle was in command of her emotions now—however temporarily—and met his enquiring glance with apparent calm.

'Right, Mrs Walpole, thanks very much. And a bottle of the *Côtes du Roussillon*, I think.'

Mrs Walpole thanked him and departed, and Gabrielle commented that the meal seemed as if it would be terrific.

'Should be. Usually is, here. The locals keep very quiet about this place—I discovered it when I was working all one holiday on the barn, and I've been coming when I can ever since. Mrs Walpole's cooking never seems to have an off-day. They're always full, of course. You have to book, or there's not a hope in hell of getting in. That's why I couldn't bring you here that Sunday, when we had lunch at the Rose & Crown.'

He'd remembered that Sunday. Gabrielle glowed.

'So I took a chance you'd be free, and rang them yesterday from London.'

Gabrielle's world spun into glory. He'd planned yesterday to bring her here.

She came down to earth with a rude jolt.

'Of course, it didn't really matter,' he added kindly. 'If you'd not been able to join me, I could always have brought Sister Cartwright, or one of the physios.'

'Of course.' She stared down at her plate with hatred. Smoked trout slid in front of her eyes, and a wedge of lemon. She picked up her knife and fork bleakly, reminding herself that he was merely being accurate. She had known it all along, hadn't she? She was one among many members of staff he'd occasionally take out for a meal to discuss work. Right. What she had to do was push away, out of her mind for ever, any nonsensical notions that there might be anything in the least special about her. She wanted to cry.

'Anything wrong with your trout?'

'No, of course not. It's lovely.' She began to eat it up fast, grinning like a maniac between mouthfuls.

The steak-and-kidney pie came, and Robert poured the wine.

Gabrielle took up yet another knife and fork and put mouthfuls of melting pastry, wonderful steak and oysters and delicious mushrooms on to a dry tongue. She chewed and swallowed, drank some wine. It tasted of vinegar. In the past few weeks, she reminded herself sternly, on her own at Bramley House, away from her usual friends and companions, mooning about the lanes, dreaming over her books in the evenings, she'd built up teenage fantasies about herself and Robert. He was her chief. Nothing else. As such, he could occasionally be approachable and even friendly, and, like Uncle Fred, he often took the staff out for dinner in a nice restaurant. A useful opportunity for uninterrupted talk about cases. Or failing the Membership. This, in fact, was very likely where he'd brought Paul for dinner that Saturday after the party, she realised with a dull ache.

'Was this where you brought Paul one Saturday?'

He looked at her, his eyes startled. 'As a matter of fact, yes, I believe I did.' She had mentioned

Paul quite deliberately, he told himself. In an attempt to remind them both exactly where they stood. Did this mean she had seen through his pretence, realised he was becoming too interested in her? Was this why she'd looked so tense earlier? Was he making her life more difficult than ever, when he wanted only to help her?

Robert too sipped a carefully chosen and expensive wine that tasted of nothing but vinegar and despair.

Mrs Walpole brought them fresh peaches covered in a purée of raspberries from the garden, a dessert so beguiling that even two frustrated lovers, embittered and morose, could hardly fail to enjoy it.

'I've never tasted anything like it,' Gabrielle said, and swallowed another delightful mouthful.

She looked happier, a little more relaxed, Robert thought. Perhaps it would be a mistake to take her up on this question of Paul. Had she meant anything by her remark, or not?

Hell, he needed to find out. Not for himself alone, either. Gabrielle's future job depended on her decision.

'When are you moving out to Ledford?' he asked baldly.

She stared at him. 'Me?'

'Who else?' Get on with it, girl, he was thinking. If I'm going to hear the worst, let's have it fast.

'L—Ledford?'

'Ledford. I believe that is the situation of the Singh practice?'

'Oh yes, it is. Of course. Sorry. It's just that—that—I may not—I'm not sure if—'

His heart leapt. She wasn't going. It was all over. Oh, my darling love, forget Paul and we'll be happy together for ever. Trust me. You'll see. 'Are you not planning to move there after all? Is that it?' he asked slowly and with extreme care, as if he might be conversing with a newly arrived Tibetan, able to comprehend only the slowest and most carefully enunciated textbook English.

She looked amazingly relieved. 'No,' she said. 'I'm not. Not for a couple of years, anyway. I—just as you said I might, I have had time to think, down here, and I came to the conclusion that you were right, everyone was right, that I shouldn't throw away the chance of a registrar's post at the Central. If I can still get one, that is.'

'You'll get one.'

'Do you think—'

'Sure of it. The same as you'll get the Membership. You didn't have a chance last time. Too much stacked against you.'

'I *ought* to have had a chance. It was my own fault.'

He shook his head. 'Not really. Circumstances were against you.' Circumstances, he thought caustically. A new name for that idiot Paul. 'You haven't finished your wine,' he said. 'Nor have I.' His heart was telling him triumphantly that he had two years, two whole years, to work on this heavenly girl and make her forget Paul. 'We'll have some cheese shall we, and finish what's left of this rather pleasant wine?' His eyes were brilliant.

She nodded. 'Be great.' Her eyes sparkled back.

Mrs Walpole brought them the cheese board, Robert ate a wedge of Stilton and Gabrielle some ripe Camembert, and the wine was mellow and smooth and nectar in her mouth.

'I'm thankful you've reached that decision,' Robert remarked, very much the director of the department, she thought. 'Because we have a meeting next week to consider appointments for the coming year, and I'd like to have my candidates all lined up.' He nodded, his curt inclination of the head giving not a clue to the pounding joy he was experiencing. 'I'll be able to include you in my list.'

'Oh, thank you.' Gabrielle was delighted. 'More than I deserve, I'm afraid. I—I hope I *do* manage to pass the Membership this time.'

He grinned cheerfully at her. 'If you don't, it's all off. But you will.'

Gabrielle crossed all her fingers and cast her eyes heavenwards.

'Not to worry.'

There was nothing for either of them to worry about, he told himself. They were going to make it. They'd have a lifetime together, he was sure of it. From now on, everything would go right for them both.

Gabrielle was thinking about two years at the Central. With Robert.

She pulled herself up sharply. He was her chief. That was all. No more fantasies.

No fantasies!

Sitting opposite him in the little green-walled, low-ceilinged dining-room, drinking the last of her wine, Robert's dark eyes meeting hers, she found it impossible not to begin to dream again.

Robert's dream was specific. He wanted to take Gabrielle back to the barn and make love to her all night, and blow the conference tomorrow. He stared at her lavender chiffon blouse, pinned at the neck with some sort of antique brooch, and all he thought about was unpinning it. The neck of the blouse had little pleats and long strips of chiffon fastened into a bow. They needed untying. The blouse, while admittedly Gabrielle looked wonderful in it, was quite extraordinarily prim, he considered. Below the stupid bow, all down the pin-tucked front where he would have liked to have had his hand, was a row of small pearl buttons.

Gabrielle could hardly fail to notice his detailed study. Unnerved, she came out of her own dreams abruptly, and squinted down her front. Had she spilt something?

That she was being undressed with a look never occurred to her.

Mrs Walpole brought their coffee, and a little dish of her own make of peppermints, *petits fours* and fondants. Gabrielle poured, and Robert, fascinated, watched her. A soft lavender chiffon arm rising in a graceful arc, the long-fingered ringless hand he knew so well holding the glass coffee jug, putting it down. The hand passed him his coffee cup.

'Thank you.' He drank scalding coffee, hoping it might bring him to his senses, and went on staring at Gabrielle. That blouse was undoubtedly one of the most unprovocative he'd come across—yet he couldn't tear his eyes away from it, nor his thoughts from dwelling on the undoing of the little pearl buttons.

The coffee, not at all to his pleasure, began to work, and he started to recognise reality again. What he had been planning was not going to happen. He couldn't take Gabrielle straight back to the barn with him. Apart from anything else, the place would be freezing cold. He'd expected on his return simply to have a quick bath and climb straight into his sleeping bag. In the morning, a mug of Nescafé and one of his apples, and he'd be on his way to the consultants' conference, which opened at ten o'clock.

A mug of Nescafé, an apple, and a two-bar electric fire. Hardly the big seduction scene.

No, it wasn't on. Everything about it was wrong. Gabrielle was involved with Paul still, and he'd sent her down here to recuperate, not to start an *affaire* with him. She was so lovely, though, his Gabrielle. And so vulnerable. He wanted to take care of her for ever.

His Gabrielle? Take care of her for ever? Unquestionably he was right out of his mind. 'Any more coffee in that pot?'

'Plenty.' Gabrielle poured again, and again Robert watched her.

Gabrielle was wondering why he'd gone so

silent. Glowering, too. He must be bored. He was used to witty, clever companions, probably, seductive and chatty, full of charm and liveliness. Not fantasising girls with nothing left to say once they'd covered the morning's clinic and the afternoon's ward round.

Robert looked at his watch. 'Better be on our way, perhaps.' He had to escape before his own urges became totally unmanageable. He had to take this girl of his back to Bramley House and then drive off himself to his unspeakable sleeping bag. 'I've got to be away early. Consultants' conference all day tomorrow.'

'Oh yes, of course. I'd forgotten.' How frightful of her. He was the chairman, too, she remembered belatedly. She ought to have been asking him about the speakers and the different papers instead of sitting here, swallowing far too many delectable *petits fours* and dreaming about nothing.

Robert paid the bill and exchanged compliments with Mrs Walpole, Gabrielle peered at her lipstick and settled Gran's shawl cosily round her shoulders. They walked back along the passage and out into the forecourt.

A fresh wind was blowing, smelling of damp soil and fallen leaves. Robert unlocked the car door, Gabrielle slid in, he shut the door and walked round to the driver's seat. He started the car, and they drove off into the darkness, back along the lanes, and into the driveway at Bramley House.

'Thank you so much for a lovely evening.'

'My pleasure.'

'Super place—incredible food.'

'We must do it again sometime,' he said easily.

Meaningless, Gabrielle told herself stoically. Or did he perhaps mean it? She had not the faintest idea.

The rear lights of his car disappeared.

Robert had gone, and she was walking slowly upstairs to her own room. The evening was over. Finished. But she knew something now. She was in love. No escaping it. In love with Robert.

She knew now what had been wrong with her feeling for Paul. It had been nothing like this. This —this whatever it was for Robert—had seized her, taken her over. It was silly and futile, and she didn't want any of it. But it was there. It wouldn't go away. It possessed her.

It had to go away. The outcome was bound to be even more of a failure than her experience with Paul. Nothing could come of it.

At this precise moment, though, whatever she told herself about the future, she felt marvellous. She was happy. Happy, it seemed ridiculously, for ever. Nothing could touch her now.

She should have known better.

CHAPTER ELEVEN

ON TUESDAY Paul rang her, suggesting they should meet at the weekend. 'You do finish at Bramley House on Saturday, don't you?'

'Yes, that's right.'

'I finish here the same day.'

She could hardly believe her ears. She'd done her own calculations with some care, and according to her reckoning he was not due to complete his two years as Robert's registrar until the end of the month. But apparently he had two weeks leave outstanding, and was to start in general practice in Ledford on the Monday. He had the weekend free, though, and suggested driving down to collect her.

'Either on Saturday or Sunday, which ever suits you.'

Offering her a choice of two days made it difficult to put him off, though she tried to do so, saying she could easily travel by train.

'But why should you, when I am free to drive down and fetch you?'

She almost insisted on catching the train, but at the crucial moment a sense of fairness stepped in. Paul had always been kind and considerate, and to imagine that she would no longer be safe in his car was ridiculous.

The trouble was only that she didn't want to

spend several hours alone with him. On the other hand, although she'd ended their engagement weeks ago, she hadn't told him their relationship was ended, that no matter what happened, she was never going to marry him. She'd told no one that. To recognise it herself had been hard enough. But before informing anyone else, she had to tell Paul. And at least if he came down to Bramley House they could be alone and uninterrupted. So she accepted his offer, saying that as she had to hand over to David Paterson on Saturday, she was not leaving until Sunday.

'If I pick you up about eleven on Sunday, then? And we could lunch somewhere nice on the way back.'

'I suppose we could,' she agreed dubiously, afraid that by the time she'd had her say neither of them would want to lunch together. Paul might even prefer to drive straight to Ledford—well, if he did, she could always go up on the train, as she'd first planned.

A solution occurred to her. 'How about having an early lunch at the Rose & Crown in South-bridge?' she suggested. 'Then Anik might be able to join us.'

'I thought we were going to be on our own for once,' Paul protested. 'I've seen nothing of you lately.'

'It would be a bit unkind, don't you think, to come down here and not see Anik? She'd be hurt, I'm sure. I'll ring her and try to fix Sunday lunch.' Take it or leave it, she thought.

Paul took it.

Anik was not on duty until two o'clock on Sunday afternoon, she said. 'It would be lovely to have lunch with you and Paul. But are you sure you are wanting me to join you?'

'Positive.' Gabrielle was decisive. She'd had time to think out her strategy, and Anik was her insurance policy. 'Paul will be here about eleven,' she explained. 'I'm going to have a talk with him in the office as soon as he arrives, to tell him about staying on at the Central for another two years. And—and other things. He's not going to like it. So it would be a great help if you joined us for lunch.'

'Oh dear, yes. I see.'

'We can drive into Southbridge, have an early lunch, and bring you back in plenty of time to be on duty at two.'

Her plan sounded all right, but she had failed to allow for Robert's appearance on Saturday morning. He'd driven David down, and he proposed, he announced, to do a round with them both and then drive Gabrielle back to London. 'Are you packed?'

'Nearly, yes. But—' What was she going to do? 'You see, I—it's terribly kind of you, but I—' Hell, why had this had to happen? If only she'd thought. But, much as she was longing to, she couldn't ditch Paul and disappear back to London with Robert. She had to face Paul and break the news to him personally that they were finished. She owed him that. Resolutely she set her lips, and embarked on her explanation. 'I'm not going up until tomorrow,' she said. 'Paul is coming down to collect me, so you see I'll—I'll have to wait until then,' she ended unhappily. This was the nearest she came to an apology, and it certainly didn't seem anything of the sort to Robert. Merely a quick brush-off.

His face darkened.

'Thank you so much for thinking of it,' Gabrielle faltered, reading his implacable expression only too easily. 'So kind of you.'

With a few casual words, she destroyed his dreams. He'd driven down like a boy in love, he told himself furiously, switching himself fiercely back into an irate consultant under pressure. 'Right.' He scowled at her. 'That's that, then. Let's get on. I haven't got all day, even if you have.'

The round, usually such a happy occasion at Bramley House, was one of the more hideous experiences of Gabrielle's life.

David's, too. 'Phew,' he sighed, as they stood together, two attentive juniors seeing the chief off. 'Thank the lord that's over. I've never known him in such a filthy mood.' The car turned out of the drive, into the lane, and disappeared. 'What on earth got into him? He was all sweetness and light on the way down. Never known him so chatty. Almost human, in fact. Well, it wore off soon enough.'

Gabrielle hardly heard what David said. Desolation had engulfed her. David made another remark she failed to catch, except that she became aware, at last, that he was standing there saying something. 'Um—what? Sorry, I was thinking.'

'I said shall we go inside and have a coffee, and then start to pick up the pieces?'

'Good idea.'

They turned and went back to the little office.

Gabrielle felt as if her heart was breaking for ever, but she pulled herself together and talked to David for hours about case papers, X-rays, diet sheets, admissions and discharges, and the characteristics of visiting parents he hadn't so far met.

The moment she woke the next morning she knew that something disastrous had happened, though she tried to reason herself out of this belief. All that had actually occurred was that Robert had brought David down, and had offered to take her back. Nothing more. When she'd explained that she wasn't leaving until today, he'd gone without her. Naturally. Hardly the end of the world. No doubt as soon as he left Bramley House, she'd ceased to exist as far as he was concerned. He forgot all about her. The only trouble was that she couldn't forget him. Well, she had to snap out of it. Instead of lying about in bed feeling miserable, she ought to be up and doing her packing, taking her books and cases down to the hall. And working out exactly what she was going to say to Paul.

From the office window, she saw the familiar Escort drive in, and went out to meet him. Both hall and drive were crowded. At Bramley House on Sunday morning, parents, brothers and sisters descended in hordes to visit. Parents' cars filled the drive. and the ten-thirty bus unloaded another large group. In the midst of all this, Gabrielle greeted Paul somewhat formally, and took him into the office.

She began her set piece. 'I'm afraid you won't like what I'm going to say. I'm sorry, Paul. but I'm not coming to Ledford.'

'This is not good news for me,' he agreed. 'But not entirely unexpected.' He was sombre.

'No?' For a moment she wondered wildly if Robert had been talking to him again, telling him he'd behaved badly.

'It is because of Anik, I see that. My own fault, as my uncle warned me. I am learning hard way that I should have taken his advice in first place, stopped her coming to UK.'

'What might have happened if Anik had not come has nothing to do with it. Now is what counts.'

'If Anik was not here, you would be coming to Ledford with me,' he said sadly.

'If Anik had not arrived, I might have passed the Membership first time, and I'd be in a different position.' Gabrielle was a little tart, but she thought she was entitled to that reminder, although, she realised for the first time, failing the Membership had changed the course of her life. And not for the worse, as it turned out. 'Anyway, I have the opportunity of two more years at the Central.' There, it was out at last.

'All this has happened because I was weak about

Anik. Whatever you said, I should have put you first. It has been lesson to me. I hope not too late.' His dark eyes were desolate. 'Be telling me it is not too late, Gaby. That in two years we will be together again.'

Almost Gabrielle weakened. Anything to take the pain out of his eyes. But she knew it was too late. What had been between them was over. 'I'm sorry, Paul. But it *is* too late. I'm not coming to Ledford. I am, if you like, putting my career first.'

Just as he would have done with a patient facing a final diagnosis, he tried again to pretend that all might yet be well. 'Once I am down in Ledford,' he said, 'I shall be in touch. We can meet on your free evenings, go out perhaps? I shall see if I can change your mind.'

'We have no future together.' Gabrielle had not intended to be so downright, but the remark slipped out before she could stop it.

'No future that we can plan at present.' Again he amended the facts to fit his own peace of mind. 'But in two years it may be different.' He put out his hand and took hers, clasped it in his own. 'I am not being able to face that all is ended, Gaby.'

Once she would have found his touch comforting. Now she snatched her hand away. At once she was ashamed. How could she be doing this to Paul? She almost reached for his hand again, took back her words. Anything to stop hurting him. Even if she knew now she could not spend the rest of her life with him, she was so fond of him, and she was longing to give in. To say, perhaps, 'All right. In a year or two we can see how we feel.' It would make him feel better, and she wouldn't really be committing herself.

It would be wrong, though. For both of them. Somehow she had to be honest. 'I'm sure,' she began tritely, 'that we shall always be friends. But we shan't be married, or living together in Ledford. Because I'm not going into general practice. I may have to move about the country, if I am ever to get a consultant post. Go anywhere I can land a job as senior registrar, and then take a consultant post wherever I can get it. I'm sorry this means making you unhappy, but I have to do it.'

'You used not to think like this.'

'No, I know. I'm sorry.'

'If you have registrar's post at Central, surely you can be seeing what you feel at the end of it? By then you may not want to travel about all over country, you might once again wish to settle down with me in Ledford.' His heart-breaking eyes searched hers, seeking the answer they desired.

Gabrielle refused to meet them. 'No, Paul. I am not going to change over this. It's too late.'

The argument continued, round and round in circles. Whatever she said, Paul managed to find some way of twisting it and wringing hope from some possibility, so that Gabrielle began to despair. Would she never be able to make him accept finality?

There was a knock on the door, and Anik's head came round it. 'Come in, come in,' Gabrielle gestured enthusiastically. She glanced at her watch thankfully. 'Time we left for lunch.'

Carrying her coat, Anik was charming in a sprigged silk sari of green leaves and vivid coral flowers, over a coral sweater. Gabrielle caught a glimpse of coral stockings below the long skirt as Anik moved gracefully forward to greet Paul. He helped her into her coat, and the three of them went out to the car, carrying Gabrielle's cases between them, and fitting them into the boot. Gabrielle then ensconced herself firmly in the back of the car, insisting that Anik sat in front with Paul. She began giving him somewhat staccato instructions on the route, while Anik told him how she and Gabrielle had been there for a meal. 'Is very pleasant hotel, Rose & Crown. You will be enjoying lunch there today, I think.'

As it was early still, Gabrielle suggested they went first to the lounge for drinks. 'I rang up and booked a table,' she said. 'For twelve-thirty, so we wouldn't have to rush, as Anik has to go on duty,'

The three of them went into the lounge.

Seated just inside the door, with a pint of bitter, the *Observer*, and a forbidding scowl, was Robert.

Gabrielle stopped in her tracks.

Anik stopped with her. Paul, however, advanced. 'Good morning, sir. Amazing luck, finding you here.'

Robert looked up, was confronted by a triangle of familiar faces. Paul, flanked by Gabrielle on one side, Anik on the other. He blinked, decided he couldn't, after all, be hallucinating. 'Morning.' He surveyed them up and down with a noticeable absence of friendliness.

Paul, however, was pleased to see his chief again. He also imagined, mistakenly, that the encounter might set a precedent for future meetings with former Central colleagues, among whom Gabrielle would naturally be numbered. Instead of the end of a relationship, the beginning of a campaign. Paul had great determination and persistence. 'May we join you, sir?'

'By all means.' Robert could hardly refuse outright, but his reply lacked warmth.

Gabrielle longed only to be somewhere else. Heaven failing to transport her to a more congenial environment, she sat gingerly down at the little table opposite Robert. His eyes encountered hers, and she saw he was blazingly angry.

Addressing the air between them, he said 'And what are you three doing here today?'

'Having lunch.' Gabrielle was short.

'I see.' Robert's anger was not directed, as Gabrielle supposed, at her, but at Paul, whom he assumed to be making her miserable yet again by dragging Anik along with them. Once too often, he decided furiously. He had spent an unhappy Saturday evening at the barn, which was bursting at the seams with all the provisions he'd brought down for what he had imagined would be a joyful weekend with Gabrielle. That had come to nothing, but enough was enough. He was going to step in and rescue his deluded Gabrielle, whether she wished it or not. 'Perhaps,' he suggested silkily, though his eyes gave the game away to Gabrielle, 'I might join you? I was intending to have lunch here.'

A polite chorus assured him that nothing could make them happier, while Gabrielle asked herself what was going on, wondering a trifle hysterically what would happen if she stood up and walked out, without explanation. She could catch the train to London, and begin life anew on Monday morning at the hospital.

Robert watched expressions—not entirely incorrectly, he read them as anxiety and misery—chase themselves across her face, and vowed to detach her finally from Paul today, if it was the last thing he did. Except, of course, that it would by no means be the last, but the first. The first step on their life together. His eyes gleamed with malevolent anticipation, and he snapped his fingers for the waiter, and began enquiring about a table for lunch.

'I booked a table,' Gabrielle interrupted. 'For three,' she added hastily, asking herself if this might be the signal for her own precipitate departure.

'Would you be so good,' Robert requested the waiter, in his grandest teaching-round manner, 'as to arrange for Dr Vereker's table for three to become one for four?'

She'd missed her opportunity. After more verbal skirmishing between Robert and an increasingly nervous trio, they moved into the dining room. Here, throughout an old-fashioned English

Sunday lunch of brown Windsor soup, roast
mutton with onion sauce, roast potatoes and cauli-
flower, followed by apple tart, Robert conducted
a high-powered symposium on childhood asthma.
Finally, as the waiter hovered enquiringly, 'Coffee
in the lounge?' he asked.

'Oh, I am so sorry, but I ought to be returning
to Bramley House. I have to be on duty at two.'
Anik cast an anguished glance at Paul.

Robert seized his opportunity. 'Right. Paul
can take you back at once. Gabrielle and I are
in no hurry, are we?' His eyes dared her to
deny this. 'We'll stay for coffee.' He nodded
to the waiter. 'Coffee for two in the lounge.
It's been delightful having you with us, Anik.
I'm glad Paul was able to bring you.' They
were all standing now, and he shook hands
formally with Anik, patting her encouragingly
on the shoulder for good measure. 'Now, Paul,
after you've taken Anik to Bramley House,
you'll want to go straight on to Ledford. I can
drive Gabrielle back to London.' This was to
pull rank in a way normally foreign to him,
but he found he had no hesitation. In fact, he
was suddenly enjoying himself enormously.

Paul was not. He gulped. 'I—er—I was going to
drive her myself.' His assertion lacked conviction.

'Right out of your way. Pointless.'

'But—'

'You take Anik, I'll take Gabrielle.'

Gabrielle opened her mouth. 'It does seem a
sensible arrangement,' she remarked, to Robert's

relief. 'My luggage is in your boot, though, Paul. I'd better come out with you and collect it.'

Robert wasn't having this. 'No need for you to go traipsing about humping luggage. Paul will see to it.' He delved into his pocket, produced car keys. 'Here you are, Paul. Put the stuff in my boot. You'll see where I'm parked, on the other side of the square, outside an antique shop.'

Paul took the keys.

'Leave them with reception,' Robert told him. 'It'll save time. Come on, Gaby, let's make for that coffee.'

Gaby. So he wasn't still annoyed with her. He only ever called her that when he was feeling friendly. For some reason she refused to analyse, she trod ecstatically back to the lounge and sat down at a little table opposite him, her eyes sparkling.

Mystified, he stared at her. 'You are the most extraordinary girl.'

She was jolted out of her trance. 'Me?' Now what?

'You come in here with a face as long as a boot —and now look at you.' He was outraged. Under the impression he'd been fighting a crusade, to save her and protect her, he'd been ready to spend both the break for coffee and the journey to London struggling to restore her shattered morale. And now look at her. Fighting fit and ready to go. Never slow in the uptake, he reached a new diagnosis fast. 'You wanted to get away from Paul.'

She nodded. That would be enough to be going

on with. Wild horses would not drag from her any sort of admission that her ecstasy was caused more by the joy of sitting here alone with Robert than by Paul's departure. 'I didn't know how on earth I was going to stand the journey back,' she explained truthfully. 'You see, I spent this morning telling Paul about my decision to stay on for another two years at the Central, and—'

'You did?' Robert's outlook spun wildly.

'Yes. I've been dreading today. I knew I had to tell Paul, so when he wanted to come down and fetch me I said yes.' She shook her head. 'But then I—I rather lost my nerve, so I persuaded Anik to come along for lunch—Paul was very cross about that, I'm afraid. And now look what we've done, on top of it.' Her eyes looked straight into Robert's, filled with guilty triumph.

'Not before time. No need to feel badly about it.'

She sighed. 'It is awful of me. I realise now I've been making use of Paul. I thought I was in love with him, when all I was looking for was a safe haven to recover from Gran's death. He was so kind always—and all I could say was that I was never going to marry him.'

'You told him that?' Robert's world exploded into brilliant searing light.

'This morning, in the office,' she said accurately. 'That's why I was dreading the drive up to London —I was even wondering if I could sort of scarper and catch the train instead.' Remembering the details of her morning, she failed to notice what had happened to Robert.

'Come on,' he said, and stood up. 'We're getting out of here.'

She looked blank. 'But—but our coffee?'

They had been too engrossed to pour it.

'To hell with the coffee. Come on.'

'But—but we've paid for it.'

'Good grief, Gaby, stop being so idiotic and come on.' Ungraciously, he hauled her to her feet.

The touch electrified her, and without another word she accompanied him out of the Rose & Crown and across the square to his car.

Her chief. More than that. Her love. Who was going to drive her to London, back to two years of work at the Central with him.

He unlocked the car, she sat down in the passenger seat, he shut the door on her and walked round to his own seat. He banged his door, started the engine, let in the clutch. They drove off.

London and the Central, here I come.

Except that they didn't seem to have turned on to the main road. They were in the lanes still. 'Where are we going?'

'The barn. Have to collect some stuff, and let the fire out.'

She was pleased. 'That'll be nice.'

His glance slid across. 'Think so?'

She nodded. 'Be great.'

They drove in and parked.

'We could have our coffee here, of course,' Robert suggested. 'There's no immense rush to reach London.' He sounded, she noticed—and for the first time ever—tentative and uncertain.

He unlocked the door and let her into the big
high-raftered room she remembered so well. The
closed stove was warm to the touch, and he opened
it up. 'Soon get ourselves a nice blaze,' he said,
stirring the red-hot embers, putting on a couple of
logs, and opening the draught inlet to its widest.

'I thought you were going to let it out.' Wasn't
that what he had specifically come here to do?

'No hurry. You stay there while I rustle us up
some coffee.' He strode off into the kitchen.

Bemused, Gabrielle sat down on a cushion by
the fire. Here she was, in the barn, in the firelight.
With Robert. Her dreams come true. This day that
she had so dreaded suddenly radiant with a rushing
unquenchable joy.

In the kitchen, filling the kettle, plugging it in,
Robert was exuberant. This weekend that had
made him so despairing had all at once flown into
wild delight, and, exactly as he had planned all
week, he had Gaby here with him in the barn.
They were alone together at last.

So what now?

Gaby must not be hurried, he informed himself
severely. He must take his time, be gentle with
her. Loving her, he reminded himself, was for a
lifetime.

With two mugs of fragrant steaming coffee, he
joined her by the fire. Little flames crept round
the logs, tendrils of sweet-smelling wood-smoke
climbed upwards, and they sipped their coffee.

Gabrielle sighed peacefully and luxuriously,
stretched comfortably. 'This is heaven,' she mur-

mured. 'And there was me thinking today was going to be so awful.'

'Awful?' He was startled.

She opened her mouth to explain about the daunting necessity to confront Paul with the unwelcome facts, but instead, to her amazement, she heard her voice say clearly and unequivocally, 'I hated not being able to go with you yesterday.'

'You did?' With enormous care he deposited his own coffee mug on the ground by the stove, removed her mug from her hands and placed it with equal care alongside it, and took her into hungry arms.

She melted into them as though she'd never belonged anywhere else, and for an eternity they kissed rapturously, thoroughly, passionately, until at last they drew back and stared incredulously at one another.

Robert's hand, that hand that Gabrielle had loved so long and so secretly, came up and smoothed her hair tenderly away from her face, touched her cheeks with—with what could only be adoration, she admitted to herself. Her own hand came up to the nape of his neck, exploring the soft skin beneath the crisply curling dark hair. 'I think I've loved you for ever,' she muttered, ashamed.

His body jerked. 'You what? Say it again.'

She said it again, loudly and with no shame at all, her heart trustingly in her eyes.

'My darling love.' He kissed her with a hard urgency he could hold back no longer, as excitement mounted in them both and they clung together recognising a new world. Momentarily, though, he leant back, away from their closeness, searched her features. 'Gaby? Would you like us to make love now?'

A spurt of irrepressible laughter broke from her. 'So what are we supposed to be doing?' she asked. She kissed him again, slowly, lingeringly, and then in her turn drew back and smoothed his brow with exultant tenderness. 'But yes, I would like us to make love now. Here, this minute.'

'Here, and for ever,' he told her.

4 Doctor Nurse Romances
FREE

Coping with the daily tragedies and ordeals of a busy hospital, and sharing the satisfaction of a difficult job well done, people find themselves unexpectedly drawn together. Mills & Boon Doctor Nurse Romances capture perfectly the excitement, the intrigue and the emotions of modern medicine, that so often lead to overwhelming and blissful love. By becoming a regular reader of Mills & Boon Doctor Nurse Romances you can enjoy SIX superb new titles every two months plus a whole range of special benefits: your very own personal membership card, a free newsletter packed with recipes, competitions, bargain book offers, plus big cash savings.

AND an Introductory FREE GIFT for YOU.
Turn over the page for details.

**Fill in and send this coupon back today
and we'll send you**

4 Introductory
Doctor Nurse Romances yours to keep
FREE

At the same time we will reserve a
subscription to Mills & Boon
Doctor Nurse Romances for you. Every
two months you will receive the latest
6 new titles, delivered direct to your door.
You don't pay extra for delivery. Postage and
packing is always completely Free.
There is no obligation or commitment –
you receive books only for
as long as you want to.

It's easy! Fill in the coupon below and return it to
**MILLS & BOON READER SERVICE, FREEPOST, P.O. BOX 236,
CROYDON, SURREY CR9 9EL.**

Please note: **READERS IN SOUTH AFRICA write to**
Mills & Boon Ltd., Postbag X3010,
Randburg 2125, S. Africa.

- -

FREE BOOKS CERTIFICATE

**To: Mills & Boon Reader Service, FREEPOST, P.O. Box 236,
Croydon, Surrey CR9 9EL.**

Please send me, free and without obligation, four Dr. Nurse Romances, and reserve a Reader
Service Subscription for me. If I decide to subscribe I shall receive, following my free parcel of
books, six new Dr. Nurse Romances every two months for £6.00*, post and packing free. If I
decide not to subscribe, I shall write to you within 10 days. The free books are mine to keep in
any case. I understand that I may cancel my subscription at any time simply by writing to you. I
am over 18 years of age.
Please write in BLOCK CAPITALS.

Name _____

Address _____

_____

_____ Postcode _____

SEND NO MONEY — TAKE NO RISKS

Remember, postcodes speed delivery. Offer applies in UK only and is not valid to present subscribers. Mills &
Boon reserve the right to exercise discretion in granting membership. If price changes are
8DN necessary you will be notified. Offer expires 31st December 1985.
* Subject to possible V.A.T.

EP15